TWO RISKS I'D NEVER TAKE AGAIN

A SWEET ROMANTIC COMEDY

NEVER SAY NEVER

BOOK SIX

REMI CARRINGTON

Two Risks I'd Never Take Again

Picking up a stranger off the side of the road is risky. Falling in love with him is . . . not going to happen. Probably.

My life is all doughnuts and sprinkles, and I can't lie to save my life.

None of that is a problem until I find a man beaten up on the side of the road. In the dark. In the rain. And even though I promised I'd never again pick up a stranger, I load him into my car—not an easy task—and drive him to a hospital. I couldn't just leave him there.

That's how I end up spending a week in a luxurious house, soaking in a hot tub, gazing at the stars, and playing nurse to Garrett. Besides the bandages and bruises, it's a recipe for romance.

Except I want no part in anything romantic. Dating will land my heart on the butchering slab, and I refuse be hurt again.

He's interested. I wish I could lie and say I'm not.

Instead, I suggest we just stay friends. What's the risk in that?

CHAPTER 1

*D*riving at night on a deserted road ignited my imagination, and numerous unlikely scenarios played out in my head. None of them good. But braving dark and empty roads was better than staying at my parents' house overnight. Loving them did not mean I enjoyed spending time with them. Mostly because of the bickering. Completely because of the bickering.

They argued constantly, and normally, I spent most of my visits clenching my teeth because of the stress. Almost every time, I left with a tension headache. Today hadn't been as bad. There'd only been one heated discussion, but today was only one day out of many.

Now I was headed back home to my quiet life of singlehood.

Between their example and my broken engagement, it was an easy decision to stay single. Love was too big a risk. And, as I'd been told, I wasn't very good at it.

Raindrops splattered on the windshield, and I shook my fist at the sky. "Just wait. I'll be home in twenty minutes. Then you can rain. Let me get home first, and I'll... um...

plant a tree somewhere." Negotiating with Mother Nature might not work, but there was no one here to say it wouldn't. "And I'll grow plants that butterflies like. Please."

I switched on the wipers. Mother Nature wasn't in a bargaining mood apparently. Or she didn't like butterflies.

The wipers slapped back and forth as the rain came down in sheets, and I squinted to see the road.

Why had I let Mom and Dad talk me into staying for the movie? I'd shown up for Thanksgiving as promised, but now I'd likely be up past my bedtime. Granted it was only a few minutes after eight, but I'd be exhausted when I woke up at four to go make doughnuts. Everyone wanted doughnuts on the busiest shopping day of the year.

The rain let up a little but didn't stop completely.

Keeping my eyes focused on the road, I felt around for my coffee and took a sip. That would help me stay alert.

Something small and fuzzy darted out into the road. I slammed on the brakes, landing coffee all over me. That stainless mug sure held in the heat. Ouch!

"You're welcome, Mr. Raccoon." I guessed at the raccoon part. That made the most sense. Whatever it was didn't hop like a bunny or skitter like an opossum or armadillo.

I pulled off to the side of the road and yanked tissues out of the center console. What a mess. I wiped my face and chest.

Lightning streaked across the sky, making it seem like daytime for a split second. In the grass, just ahead, something moved. I stared out, scanning the area lit by my headlights.

An arm! And it had to be attached to a body because it was moving.

With my eyes squeezed closed, I grabbed the steering wheel and counted to ten. If the arm was some sort of hallucination, when I opened my eyes, it would be gone. And I'd never trust Mom to make coffee again.

Prying my eyes open one at a time, I leaned forward.

The arm moved again.

I wasn't hallucinating. Bad coffee and too much turkey weren't to blame. There was a body on the side of the road. This wasn't even one of the scenarios I'd thought of, but this was scarier than all of those scenarios. This was what nightmares were made of.

I needed to call Eli. My cousin would know what to do. He'd been trained to know what to do. The first thing he'd tell me was to stay in my car. This could be a trap. I scanned the area again. Was there some burly guy hiding out of sight, waiting to grab me as soon as I jumped out to investigate?

After a deep breath, I picked up my phone. Eli would want me to call 911. I'd call him second.

My hands shook as I tapped the screen, but nothing happened. All those stupid games I'd played during the movie had run my battery down. Of course, the one time I found a body on the side of the road, my phone was dead.

The last time I'd picked up a stranger off the side of the road, she'd thrown up in my car. Eli had lectured me until my ears hurt, and my car smelled horrid. I'd sworn never to risk doing that again. And I bought seat covers. Lesson learned.

But I couldn't drive off and leave this poor person in the ditch. That would be heartless.

As I tried to figure out what to do, the arm kept moving back and forth.

Raindrops continued to pound on the car. And the person.

If I left whoever it was in the ditch, they could drown or freeze. It wasn't below freezing, but it was cold. Did it have to be freezing for hypothermia to set in? I had to risk helping the person.

With my umbrella open, I stepped out, watching for the

burly guy as I walked toward the body. The umbrella could double as a weapon if anyone jumped out of the darkness. With my coat pulled tight around me, I shivered as I tiptoed toward the figure. The headlights made the body easy to spot.

I leaned over the man, blocking the rain from hitting his face with my umbrella. "Hello, are you okay?"

What a stupid question! How many people napped on the side of the road in the dark and in the rain?

He grabbed my ankle.

The scream that echoed through the night was mine. But the biggest shocker was that I stayed upright and didn't land on my butt. "Okay, so maybe warn me before you do that. Please."

He let go. His eyes were nearly swollen closed. Blood dribbled out of his mouth and was caked to spots on his cheeks. The rain hadn't washed it all away.

"I need to get you to the hospital." I glanced back at my car. "I'm going to pull up closer, but I promise not to run over you."

His head moved back and forth. And his mouth moved.

"What?" I dropped to my knees.

This was a bad idea.

He gripped my wrist and tugged me closer. And to my credit, I squelched my scream before making the man go deaf. He tried speaking again, but I couldn't understand him. One thing was clear—he was in a lot of pain.

I wiped at one of the spots of blood the rain hadn't washed away. "I'd never forgive myself if I left you here, and I don't even know you. But you can't tell anyone. If Eli—he's my cousin and a deputy—if he finds out I picked up a stranger again, he will never stop lecturing me." I shoved the handle of the umbrella into his hand. "Hold this, and that will make it easier not to hit you. Be right back." I slipped in the mud as I tried to get up and nearly landed on top of him. That would've been awkward. And painful for him.

When I found my footing, I ran back to my car. Good thing I had seat covers because my backside was covered in mud. Clutching the wheel, I wanted to do breathing exercises to calm down, but this guy was in bad shape. There wasn't time for slow breathing and counting to twenty.

I shifted into drive and focused on the umbrella. Inching forward with my car, I pulled as close as I dared.

After opening the passenger door, I scanned the area again checking once more for a delayed burly-guy attack. There was no one hiding in the shadows and no one to help me get the injured man into my car. I'd have to figure out a way to do it alone.

"Okay, so now is the fun part. I have to get you into my car." I dropped down to my knees and pressed a finger to his neck.

He was so still, I wanted to feel that blood was still pumping through his veins. But he was still holding the umbrella, so likely he wasn't dead. Yet.

I needed to hurry. "Before we do this, I feel like I should introduce myself. I'm Tessa. And normally I don't put my hands all over strangers."

He was probably rolling his eyes at me, but they were closed, so I couldn't confirm that.

After tossing the umbrella aside—I could grab it after he was in the car—I pulled his arm around my shoulders. He responded with a moan. When I reached over and grabbed his other hand, the moan changed to a scream.

I fell backward. "I'm so sorry. Now I know not to touch that arm."

He reached out with his one good arm, and I grabbed his hand.

"I'll make this work. I won't leave you here." I moved close to his head. "I'm going to see if I can get your head up and then drag you to my car." Squatting, I lifted his head and shoulders until I managed to get my arms around him.

His reaction was what I'd expect from someone suffering agonizing pain.

Yanking on him and sliding in the mud, I let go after only a few inches. "That's not working. I need a different plan." I knelt beside him, and he hooked his arm around my shoulders. "Okay, good. You hold onto me, and I'm going to wrap my arms around your middle. If you need me to let go, just scream." I accepted his nod as an agreement to my plan.

But it wasn't a very good plan.

I slid my hands under him and hoped with everything in me that the reason his shirt was wet was because of the rain and not because he was severely wounded and blood had been pooling beneath him. If I loaded him into my car and he died on the way to the hospital, I'd have a lot of explaining to do.

With my hands clasped together behind him, I tried to stand, lifting with my legs. But my legs weren't prepared for this. I ended up on my back with the bloody stranger on top of me. This was bad. One thing wasn't so bad—we were closer to the car.

"Okay, so that didn't go like I planned. But I learned two things. I need a different plan, and you are built like a brick." I didn't have the muscle for this.

He clearly did but was in no shape to be of much help.

"How am I going to do this?"

He shifted as his feet moved.

"Are you trying to stand up?"

His head bobbed slightly.

"Okay. New plan number whatever. Who's counting? I'm going to help you stand up, and then you can walk to my car. Maybe." I pressed on his chest. "Oh wow, you've got some muscle. I'm going to need you to help get your big muscles off me at least enough for me to move."

He was probably nice to look at without a shirt, but that thought wasn't going to get us any closer to the car.

With his good arm, he pushed up, giving me just enough room to maneuver. Thinking about how much muscle was in that one arm was just another bunny trail I didn't need to follow. But I kept thinking about how the man would look without a shirt, which was a major distraction.

"I'm going to flip over and try lifting you up enough so that you can get your feet underneath you." I rolled to my stomach. "Hang on as best as you can."

Sloshing in mud, I pushed up to my hands and knees. He had one arm wrapped around me, and I inched up higher.

He shifted and wiggled, and I hoped he'd get his footing.

Thunder clapped as lightning flashed, and we both landed in the mud, me on my stomach and the man on his back not far from me.

He covered his face with his good arm. Seeing his torment made it hard—impossible, rather—not to sob. But sobbing made it hard to communicate. After a deep breath, I squashed the sobs. Mostly.

Sniffling, I tried to act brave. "I think we almost had it. Let's give it another go."

He lifted his arm, and I suspected he was looking at me.

I crawled through the mud and stopped beside him. "So, Mr. Chiseled Brick, we're going to do that all over again. And I'm sorry for acting like we're mud wrestling. I know it's hurting you." If I kept talking, I'd start sobbing again.

Somehow, with his arm strength and my stubbornness, we ended up with him on top of me. Again. This time when I used my back to get him partially upright, he didn't slip.

"Whoa! You can stand." I scrambled to my feet. "Now I

know you're a *tall* chiseled brick." I pointed at my car as I walked. "Don't worry about the mud. I have seat covers."

He didn't move. Well, he sort of wobbled in place, and I rushed to his side before we had to start the whole process over again.

I tucked an arm around him. "Hang onto me."

After draping an arm around my shoulders, he slumped against me. He could walk, but he needed my help. This was easier than dragging him.

Every step drew out another moan, and when he dropped into the passenger seat, the rain stopped—probably because Mother Nature hated me—and I was crying. Again.

I made my living feeding people doughnuts. Causing pain was the opposite of that, and I hated it.

"I am so sorry." I reached around him and buckled the seat belt.

He brushed at a tear on my face.

The overhead light let me really see him for the first time, and I noticed the tears in his eyes. I could barely see his eyes because of how swollen they were, but sparkling in the little slits were tears. Or maybe that was rain. I could pretend it was rain. But those were tears.

"I don't mean to cry, but I can't help it. I've always been a sympathy crier. And you were moaning." I needed to shut up and get the man to the hospital. "Please forgive me for hurting you."

He cupped a hand to my cheek, and there was a pull of familiarity about him. But I didn't have time to figure that out right now.

Instead of jerking away, I leaned into his hand a second. "I hope that means you forgive me."

He tapped once with his thumb.

"One for yes. Two for no?"

Another tap seemed like an answer.

"Good. That will help us." I ran around and climbed into the driver's seat. "There's a county hospital not too far from here. We'll go there." It meant backtracking, but at least I knew where I was headed. "So if you are up to it, let's play a little game. I don't think you should go to sleep because—just don't, okay?"

He moaned.

"Good. Anyway, the game. I'll say the alphabet slowly. You let me know when I get to the first letter of your name." I turned off the wipers and eased back onto the road, keeping to a steady speed and avoiding bumps and potholes as best I could. I didn't want to torture the man. "A... B... C... D..."

The alphabet seemed much longer when a dying man occupied the passenger seat. Maybe he wasn't dying. I hoped he wasn't dying.

"E... F... G..." I continued through the alphabet, and when I hit the letter T, I wondered if maybe he'd missed the point of the game. "U... V... W... X—"

He grabbed my arm.

"What?" I slammed on the brakes, and he moaned again but louder than the last time. Stopped in the middle of the road, I flipped on the overhead light. "Is something wrong?"

His mouth moved like he was trying to speak. But even the small movement sparked fresh tears in his eyes. The whole time, his hand stayed on my arm. Then he tapped twice.

"Two for no, right? Okay. So, nothing is wrong. Wait. Were you trying to signal me?"

He tapped once.

"Okay. Sorry. I'm a little on edge. Your name starts with X." I started driving again. "Okay, hmmm. Xavier?" I shot him a side glance.

He tapped twice on my arm.

"Not Xavier. Xander?"

9

I felt two more taps.

"I don't know of any other X names." I was out of ideas. "I guess the game wasn't a great idea."

After several silent minutes, the hospital came into view. I'd never been so relieved. I was also pleased that we weren't in the same county where my cousin worked. He was less likely to find out that I'd picked up a stranger on the side of the road. Again. Unless I told him, which I had no plans to do. But that also meant not telling my best friend who was engaged to my cousin.

I wasn't great at lying, but I could keep a secret. Probably. "We're almost there."

My passenger squeezed my arm.

I turned in and pulled up to the emergency entrance. "I'll be right back."

He didn't let go of me.

Under the bright lights at the entrance, I could see just how badly he'd been hurt. The way he looked at me stoked the spark of familiarity and transformed it into a raging fire, but my thoughts were too scattered to remember how I knew him or where I'd seen him.

I rested my hand on his. "I'm going inside to get help. But if you want me to stay for a little while, I can do that."

He tapped once before pulling his hand away. Not only was his face messed up, but his hand was also. And that was his good hand. I was afraid to find out what was wrong with his other arm.

Why had I promised to stay? At this rate, I wouldn't get any sleep before it was time to make the doughnuts.

CHAPTER 2

The mystery man made a whimpering sound as hospital staff loaded him onto a gurney. They called out visible injuries, but my brain couldn't absorb what they were saying. I felt horrible for this injured man. What did he look like when he wasn't impersonating a punching bag? Who was out there wondering where he was? Surely someone missed him. It was Thanksgiving night.

Why was he so familiar?

"Don't touch his right arm. That hurts him. A lot." I hovered close, worried about the poor stranger.

When he reached out his hand, I moved in closer. "They're going to help you, okay?"

He clasped my hand, and I was careful not to touch what looked like road rash on the back of his knuckles.

I ran along side, keeping up as they pushed through the double doors.

The nurse waved a hand in front of my face. "Ma'am, what's his name?"

Based on her frustrated expression, I gathered it wasn't the first time she'd asked. But it was the first time I'd heard.

"I don't know. I tried to play a game where he signaled when I got to the first letter of his name, and that was X. But he shook his head when I asked if his name was Xavier or Xander. So, I don't know."

She glanced down at his hand wrapped around mine. "You don't know him?"

I shrugged. "I don't recognize him, but…" I widened my eyes and nodded at him, hoping she'd understand that his battered face hindered recognition. I didn't want him to hear me say how bad he looked. That seemed unkind.

The nurse looked at him. "What's your name?"

Even though she wasn't talking to me, I answered. "I'm Tessa. He can't really talk." That seemed pretty obvious, but I said it anyway.

She ignored me. "Is there anyone we can call for you?"

The guy let go of my hand and pointed at me.

It made no sense why he was appointing me guardian or whatever his pointing meant, but maybe he thought of me as his guardian angel. A muddy, sympathy-crying guardian angel.

I stepped out of the way as they wheeled him into the back but leaned around the nurses and called after him, "I'll see you later."

Too muddy to sit in a chair, I paced. But after only two laps around the room, a woman motioned me toward the big glass check-in window. "Could you please fill these out for him?"

"I don't know him. I spilled coffee on myself and pulled over. And I found him on the side of the road." I wrapped my arms around myself. "He looks familiar though."

Her brow furrowed as she gave me a surveying look. "The police will want you to answer a few questions."

"Okay." It wasn't a surprise that the police would be called. And like it or not, I was involved, but I was a mess. I didn't want to leave, but I needed clean clothes. "I'm going to run out to my car. If he asks for me, tell him I'll be right back."

"I thought you didn't know him." She tapped her pen against the desk.

"I don't, but I want to know he's okay." I pointed outside. "I'll be right back. Is there a restroom in here?"

She pointed to a hall. "Down that way on the left."

"Thanks." I moved my car out of the drop-off lane and into a parking space, which I should've done as soon as they'd rolled him through the doors.

Grateful that I'd packed a just-in-case bag to take to my parents' house, I grabbed clothes and found the restroom. There wasn't much to be done about the mud in my hair, so I knotted it atop my head and shed my muddy clothes. Clean clothes felt like a luxury. The dirty clothes got wrapped in the ruined seat covers and dropped into my trunk.

Wringing my fingers, I walked to the far corner of the waiting area, plugged in my phone to charge, and curled up in a chair. As my adrenaline rush waned, my eyelids grew heavy. A few minutes of sleep would probably do me some good.

When my eyes closed, I saw the stranger's face. Familiarity clawed at me. I knew him.

That thought made me sick. Seeing a stranger in pain was bad enough.

"Ma'am." A man's voice sounded close.

I sprang out of the chair, nearly crashing into a wall of a man in uniform. "Yes?"

He backed up, surprise sparking in his brown eyes. "I didn't mean to startle you. I'm Deputy Gomez."

"Not your fault. I'm a bit jumpy tonight."

"Would you like to walk next door and grab a cup of coffee? We can talk there." He shifted his belt.

Was he flirting or just playing the good cop? I was in no mood to meet the bad cop tonight.

"I don't want to leave." I glanced at the doors where they'd wheeled my new friend out of sight.

"Okay." Deputy Gomez nodded slowly and pulled a small notebook out of his shirt pocket. "Can you tell me what happened? We have a guy badly beaten with no ID, and you brought him in."

"He was on the side of the road. I found him like that. I've already told this to multiple people." I crossed my arms and tried to keep my voice even.

"Did he say anything to you?"

"He just moaned a lot. I tried to figure out his name, but he may have been too hurt to understand because he signaled on X, and then tapped no when I asked if his name was Xavier or Xander. What other X names are there?"

"Tapped no?" The deputy scribbled in a tiny notebook.

"One for yes. Two for no. Isn't that like some universal code?" I glanced toward the double doors. "Can I see him?"

With a furrowed brow, the deputy looked up from his notes. "I thought you didn't know him."

"I didn't. Don't. Maybe. Whatever. But after rolling around in the mud together, we sort of have a bond. I need to know that he'll be okay." I wouldn't be able to sleep until I knew he'd survive, and trying to explain to the deputy that the man looked familiar would only use up perfectly good air.

Deputy Gomez surveyed my outfit. "The mud?"

"I changed." I gave a shrug, not interested in explaining how I'd managed to get the stranger on his feet. "I was driving home from my parents' house—because it's Thanks-giving—and I spilled coffee on myself thanks to an animal that ran across the road. I pulled over to wipe my face, and that's when I spotted the guy. My phone was dead so I couldn't call anyone. It's cold outside, and he doesn't even have a jacket, so I loaded him into my car and drove him here." I sighed when I finished. "That's what happened."

He tapped the pen against the little notepad. "So... you maybe don't know him but loaded him into your car and brought him here. And now you're waiting for... what?"

"I slammed on my brakes to avoid hitting a small fuzzy animal. Do you think I'd just drive away and leave an actual person on the side of the road? As to why I'm waiting... do you only read half a mystery? I'd like to know if he's going to be okay and maybe find out what happened."

"Picking up a stranger was risky."

"You sound like my cousin."

"Who's your cousin?"

Lightbulbs went off in my head before I made my situation worse. "Doesn't matter."

A nurse with silver hair and an efficient smile walked out of the double doors, headed straight for me. "Miss."

"Yes?" I stepped around the deputy.

"He's asking for you." She hooked a thumb over her shoulder.

I picked up my purse and phone. "He's talking?"

"Trying to. But he keeps pointing this direction. It wasn't hard to figure out what he wants. And, Deputy Gomez, just let me know if you need to talk to the patient again."

"Thanks." The deputy put his hand on my arm. "I need to get your name and a contact number. And if you think of anything else that might help, please call me." He held out a card.

I gave him my info, then followed the nurse to the back.

She pulled aside a curtain and motioned for me to go in. "I pulled a chair in for you."

Pillows were tucked in around the guy's head, and the top of the bed was lifted. He was bare-chested, but a sheet covered his lower half. A brace was on one hand and the other was wrapped in bandages. Only his thumb stuck out the side of the brace. The other hand was completely wrapped.

He looked horrible.

I flashed a smile, determined to be a bright spot if possible. "Hey there, Mr. X." I froze as my own words bounced around in my head.

Last month, I'd called a guy Mr. X after I'd turned him down for a date. I'd emphatically told him that I couldn't know his name. He'd met with Eli and was probably part of some surprise for Delaney that Eli was cooking up. I'd told him I didn't want to know because if Delaney asked me about anything, I couldn't lie convincingly.

The guy in the doughnut shop that day had been strikingly handsome. Fan-myself-and-sigh kind of handsome.

I blinked after staring at him too long. "I've met you, haven't I?"

His thumb tapped the bed once.

The chair screeched as I dragged it closer to the bed. I slid my hand under his. "You were in the doughnut shop a few weeks ago."

He tapped my hand. Just once.

"You asked me out."

The thumb brushed my hand again about the same time one of my tears landed on the bed. I pictured how he'd looked before someone pummeled his face.

"You told me X so that I wouldn't know your name, huh?"

That thumb answered.

"I know I said I didn't want to know your name, but now I need to know your name. Don't you want me to tell your family that you're okay?"

He tapped twice.

"What about Eli?" Offering that was a risk because then

I'd have to come clean about what I'd done.

Another two taps let me off the hook.

"If you want me to stay, I need to know your name." I could be bossy if need be.

The thumb moved back and forth. He wasn't answering, just caressing my hand.

"Please. It'll help clear things up with the deputy who thinks I'm crazy for picking up a stranger on the side of the road."

The nurse walked in. "If we can get his info, we can send him home with a prescription for something a bit stronger. He's probably in quite a bit of pain." She set a clipboard down. "So, if you can get any info, that would be helpful." Clearly, the curtains didn't block the sound.

"Why can't he talk?"

She glanced at the bed, and my mystery man nodded. "He's got a case of vocal fatigue, it looks like."

"Vocal fatigue?" I blinked away tears as the realization hit. "You yelled for help for a while?"

The tap felt more like another caress. He knew I was about to cry again.

"Okay. You let your vocal cords rest, and we'll get this paperwork filled out. Deal?"

His thumb brushed my hand again.

I shouldn't like the way it felt. "First name. A... B... C... D... E..." I snuck a glanced at his chest. It was obvious why he felt like a brick on top of me. "F... G..."

The tap stopped me.

"G." I wrote in the first letter of his first name. This was going to take a while. "Next letter of the first name. A..."

He gave the signal.

"G A. Hmm. You don't look like a Gary or a Gandalf. If you were Gandalf, you'd have a cool staff and a few hobbits following you around."

He shifted and winced.

"Sorry. Let me think. Gabe or Gabriel?"

Nope.

"Gavin?" I kept my hand under his. "Not Gavin. You aren't named Gallagher, are you?"

Two taps brushed against my hand.

"Garrett?" When he tapped once, I grinned. "Yay! It's nice to meet you, Garrett, who likes my pecan praline doughnuts. One T or two at the end?"

He gave the signal, and I filled out his form one-handed.

"I hope your last name is short. Should I start at A?"

His head moved back and forth as he double tapped.

"I think you just want to see if I can say the alphabet backward." I wouldn't do well if I were ever pulled over for drunk driving because I could barely handle backward ABCs sober. "Z... Y... X... W..."

After he signaled, I moved onto the next letter. We continued the game until I'd filled in Garrett Wright. I stared at what I'd written. Where had I heard that name?

He shifted his head to look at me. His eyes were blue. I could tell now that the swelling had gone down a bit. Blue eyes. With my eyes closed, I thought back to that day in the doughnut shop when he'd asked me out. He'd seemed familiar then even though I'd never met him. He reminded me of someone.

Garrett brushed his thumb on my hand.

"Sorry. I was trying to figure out why you seem familiar."

His mouth moved, but his words were soft.

I stood and leaned over the bed. "What?"

"Beau Henry."

Hovering inches over Garrett, I stared at him. "You're Beau's son."

His brace bumped my shoulder. Only once. Everyone in town knew Beau Henry.

"I should call him. Eli will know how to get a hold of him."

Garrett shook his head and tapped my shoulder twice.

"All right. We'll just go back to filling out this form. If you feel up to whispering, it might go faster."

"Yes." His face twitched like he was trying to smile.

When Garrett had shown up in town just over a year ago, Beau's secret son was gossiped about a lot. From everything I knew, Beau and his family were good and kind. Why wouldn't Garrett want them to know about what happened?

In two hours, I was supposed to start making doughnuts. I was beginning to question if I'd make it there on time.

Once I had the form filled out and delivered to the nurses, I sat in the chair by Garrett's bed. "Where are your clothes?"

He pointed to a bag at the foot of his bed.

I pulled out his shirt and jeans, hoping I could clean them up enough for him to at least make it home. His shirt was cut down the middle. He wouldn't be wearing that again. His jeans were caked with mud.

"You keep acting like you want to leave, but you don't have anything to wear. Unless you want to walk out of here in boots and a hospital gown." I glanced at the sheet. "And whatever's under that sheet."

He motioned me closer. "If you go to the store, I'll pay you back." Slowly, his voice was regaining strength, but I didn't want him to overdo it.

"I would go to the store except it's one in the morning, and nothing is open. A little creativity is required."

"My house."

"I don't mind taking you to your house, but what are you going to wear on the way? Because like that you'd be cold, and I'd have trouble focusing on the road." Gosh, I was tired. "I didn't mean to say that last part out loud."

He rested the brace on my hand. "You go while people are asleep."

"I am *not* going to sneak into a house where people are sleeping. I'll get shot!"

"I live alone. In a cabin. You won't be noticed." His thumb brushed my hand. "Please."

Nodding, I picked up my purse. "I'm probably going to regret this. And don't bother making a list because I'm only grabbing jeans and a shirt. That's it."

"Thanks."

"And when I get back, I want you to tell me what happened. Who did this to you?"

His eyes narrowed. "Maybe."

"That sounded a lot like 'later' to me. I'm agreeable to that. Now tell me where I'm supposed to go."

With detailed directions, complete with landmarks visible in the dark, I drove to the ranch. I slowed down as I pulled through the gate as if that would make me harder to see. When I reached the fork in the road, I followed his directions, hoping I was remembering correctly. Three cabins came into view, and I breathed a sigh of relief.

Avoiding the first cabin, so I didn't wake the woman who lived there, I rolled to a stop in front of the third cabin. He said it wouldn't be locked, and he was right.

Stomping on my curiosity, I avoided the temptation to snoop around the place. In the bedroom, I grabbed a pair of jeans off the floor and picked the softest T-shirt out of the drawer.

I returned to the car and drove back toward the gate, hoping police didn't show up at my door tomorrow to arrest me for breaking and entering.

I hadn't broken anything. I'd just entered. Was that a crime?

CHAPTER 3

*W*hen I arrived back at the hospital, Garrett was talking loud enough to be understood by everyone. "When can I get out of here?" He glanced at me as I stepped into the curtained area, then focused on the nurse.

She shook her head. "This isn't a prison. I'll get the doctor and see about discharge papers."

"You are in such a hurry to leave, but you don't want anyone at the ranch to know you're hurt. You baffle me." I set his clothes at the foot of the bed. "Here are your clothes."

"Tessa."

I froze, remembering how he'd shocked me that day in the doughnut shop when he'd said my name. "Yeah?"

"You've done so much to help me, but can I ask for one more favor?" He held out his brace.

I put my hand on it, resting the side of my finger against his thumb. "What do you need?"

"When they release me, will you drive me somewhere?"

"That's it? That's the big favor?" I needed to stop letting this guy hold my hand. I just didn't want to stop because it felt nice. "Of course I'll drive you."

His thumb moved back and forth, ramping up the nice feelings. "Thanks."

"I'll wait for you out there, in the waiting room. Hopefully the nurses can get you dressed."

His nurse walked around the curtain. "I'll help him." She didn't look like she minded all that much. Maybe she was ready to be rid of him.

Thirty minutes later, for the second time in one night, Garrett was helped into the passenger seat of my car. At least this time, it wasn't me loading him into the car.

The seat covers were in my trunk, and I didn't have even a glimmer of hope they'd ever come clean.

Instead of rushing to the shop to make the doughnuts, I was helping Garrett. But only until I took him where he wanted to go. Then I'd race to the shop and figure something out. Hopefully.

"Okay, Mr. Stubborn, where am I taking you?" My lack of sleep had my normal filter on the fritz.

He reached across and touched my arm. "Thank you for everything. Just take me to a hotel."

I glanced at his bare chest. "I brought you a shirt."

"Sorry to be a distraction. My shoulder hurts too much to get a T-shirt on right now."

I adjusted the heat to keep him warm enough. Just the sight of him without a shirt kept me warm enough. "Regarding the hotel idea, are you crazy? You have a prescription that needs to be filled. And you'll continue wincing every time you take a deep breath until you get those meds in you. Besides that, how are you planning to eat?"

"I'll order out."

"Let me point out that you can't use your hands. Are you planning to have the delivery guy feed you? That wouldn't be weird at all." I rubbed my temples. "And weren't you listening when the doctor said to make sure someone stayed with you because you might have a concussion?"

"I forgot about that." His shoulders sagged, and he leaned his head back.

"One more minor, teeny tiny point. You have no wallet. How do you plan to pay for the hotel, food, and whatever else?"

His eyes closed, which made me feel bad.

"I didn't mean to yell at you, but I don't know why you are so set on not telling anyone at the ranch what's going on."

He sighed and grimaced. "My dad is away on his honeymoon. Finally. I almost ruined his relationship with Lilith once, and I refuse to be the reason he has to cut his trip short. Everyone at the ranch would gladly help me. They'd also call him. He'll be home in a week. I can survive that long." Garrett folded his arms across his chest, which showed off his biceps, but that treat only lasted a second. After a grimace, he dropped his arms into his lap.

"Shoulder?"

"Yeah. But it should start to feel better now that everything is where it's supposed to be."

"One week?"

He nodded.

Growing up, I'd learned to trust people based on two things—their family and their actions. Most of the time, kind people raised kind people. And while small-town rumors could sometimes be awful, they sometimes spread truth. I'd learned that the hard way. Beau Henry was as good as they came, and everything I'd heard about Garrett made it seem like he was as good and kind as his dad.

The fact that I liked the way it felt to have Garrett brush his thumb along my hand had nothing—absolutely nothing— to do with my decision. Probably.

I shifted into drive. "All right. I know where you can go, but I have to make a quick stop on the way."

He stayed quiet as I drove toward Stadtburg. If I hurried, it would still be dark when we got to town. I stole a glance at the man beside me. His eyes were closed, but his pain was still obvious.

As I passed the spot where I'd picked him up, I slammed on the brakes.

"Sheeeeeeets and towels! Are you *trying* to inflict pain?" He peered at me through one open eye. "Please don't do that again."

"I didn't mean to hurt you." I eased off the road. "I remembered my umbrella. I like that one."

I ran to the side of the road, using my phone's flashlight to avoid stepping in large patches of mud and tripping in the dark. When I picked up the umbrella, I saw the wallet next to my tire tracks.

After struggling to fold the umbrella, I tossed it into the back seat half open. Hopefully, it wasn't bad luck to have an umbrella open in a car. Did half closed make the luck less bad?

"I think I found your wallet." I held it out to him.

He looked at the wallet, then at his bandaged and braced hands.

"Right, Sorry." I opened it and pulled out the ID. "The picture doesn't look like you right now, but it has your name on it."

"Thanks. Now you can—"

"Don't even say it." I dropped the wallet into the cup holder and started driving. "All the other reasons for not going to a hotel still apply."

If I went much longer without sleep or food, I'd be a monster. After dropping him off, I had to go get his prescription filled, but the closest all-night pharmacy was in San Antonio.

I could stay awake a while longer. I had to.

When we arrived in town, the sun was just spreading light across the horizon. Usually, I loved the glimmer of daybreak. Today it taunted me.

"Wait here. I'll be right back." I parked in front of the doughnut shop. Inside, I grabbed a sheet of paper from the supply room. I knew what I wanted to do; I just wasn't sure what to write on the sign.

With my eyes squeezed closed, I forced my brain to focus. Then I scribbled on the page.

On vacation this week. Sorry for the inconvenience.

I taped it to the front window, then locked the store. For the first time since Skeeter had called off our wedding, I closed my shop.

Before I even started the engine, Garrett spoke. "Don't close. I never intended for you to do all this, and I can't let you—"

I put my hand up, then waggled a finger in his face. "Let me? I am capable of making my own decisions. Thank you very much."

His eyebrows lifted, but he didn't say a word.

The hum of the engine was the only noise as I drove to my apartment.

"Let's get you inside before someone sees you." I opened his door and helped him out. "Once you're settled, I'll go get your prescription."

He followed me down the walkway to my apartment door. "Sleep first."

I wasn't sure I'd be able to sleep. After the doctor had warned that Garrett could potentially have a concussion, I worried that he'd go to sleep and never wake up. "Maybe."

He moved at a snail's pace, understandably.

When he headed toward the sofa, I grabbed his arm. "No. That won't work. Eli or Delaney will show up when they see that the shop is closed. You can stretch out in my room."

I piled the pillows and pulled back the covers.

As he moved toward the bed, I noticed the mud still caked in his hair. It would get all over the bed, and being dirty couldn't possibly be comfortable. "Change of plans."

He stopped in the middle of the room. "What?"

"I know I can't get the bandages wet, but your hair is a mess. Hang on just a sec, while I think."

Shaking his head, he glanced at the bathroom.

"I'm not giving you a shower. We'll deal with that later." Hopefully never.

His jeans rode low on his waist, and combined with the lack of a shirt, he made it hard to think clearly. Or at all. Would it be rude to pull his jeans up a little? Why hadn't the nurse put on his belt?

"This is what we're going to do. The kitchen sink has a spray nozzle." I ran to the kitchen and set a chair in front of the sink. He was tall enough to sit in the chair with his head tilted back and be over the sink.

I hurried back to the bedroom. "Put your arm around me, and I'll help you over there. "It's probably good that you don't have a shirt on."

"Good for whom exactly?"

"Just sit and be quiet." I tucked a throw pillow behind his back and a towel behind his neck so he wouldn't hurt being in the chair. "Let me grab my shampoo." As I walked to the bathroom, I gave myself a pep talk. Washing his hair wasn't weird. That was a lie. It was very weird, but I'd do it anyway. He couldn't sleep with mud flaking out of his hair, and I didn't want mud all over my bed.

He tipped his head back as I walked toward the sink. "Am I going to smell like flowers?"

"More like mint chocolate chip ice cream." I turned on the faucet and wet his hair, running my fingers through it to shake out the mud.

He closed his eyes and gave a contented sigh.

Now it was awkward.

I massaged in the shampoo, careful not to get it near his eyes or bandages, then made sure the water was warm and rinsed out the soap. With a dishtowel, I dried his hair a little. "That should feel at least a little better. You can't shower until tomorrow."

"Thank you. That felt nice."

I wiped drips off his shoulders and chest. "Off to bed with you."

He shuffled down the hall, then dropped onto the edge of the bed.

"Your boots. I can help you." I'd never taken off a man's boots before. Was it better to face him and pull or to face away? I opted for away.

His chuckle made me think that wasn't the best choice. Most of my choices tonight had been questionable.

I carried his boots out to the kitchen so that they wouldn't leave any more flecks of dried mud on my carpet.

As I walked back into the room, he shifted into place, his jaw clenched. I covered him but hesitated to walk away. Would watching him keep him alive?

"Tessa, you can get the meds later. Sleep for a bit."

"I'll wait until the closest pharmacy opens. But I have to eat first. You hungry?"

"Starved, but I'm not sure what I can eat right now. Even talking hurts."

"Then quit talking. I didn't know it was hurting you. I'll bring you something to eat." I walked out, forcing myself not to look back. At least now I could honestly say I hadn't picked up a stranger.

I just didn't know that when I'd loaded him into my car.

In the kitchen, I heated a pan and quickly scrambled some eggs, making sure they were light and fluffy. He could down those without having to chew.

When I ran to the pharmacy, I'd get puddings and Jell-O. For lunch, maybe I'd whip up a creamy soup.

With food loaded onto a tray, I walked back into the bedroom. "Okay, G-man. Let's get some food in you."

"You first." He closed his mouth, looking very much like a toddler refusing vegetables.

I shoveled eggs into my mouth, then swallowed before scolding him. "For someone completely at my mercy, you sure like to pretend you're in charge." I piled eggs on a clean fork. "Now, open up."

He opened his mouth as best he could and practically inhaled the food.

"You *were* hungry." I wiped his mouth, dusting away a few crumbs.

His gaze tracked my movements, and I swallowed. One week. I'd help him for one week, and then he could go back to his life, and I'd go back to mine.

"Try to sleep." I picked up the tray and nestled a bag of frozen peas onto his face. "After you're a bit more rested, we'll call the deputy from last night so you can tell him what happened."

"I will not. He knows what he needs to know. I had an unfortunate mishap, and I don't wish to press charges. When you went to get clothes, he came back. I talked to him."

I set the tray down and perched on the edge of the bed. "What happened?"

With the bag of peas covering half his face, he stared at the far wall, and for the better part of a minute, I thought he wasn't going to answer me.

"Someone jumped me and beat me up."

"That clears it all up for me. Thanks." I picked up the tray.

"Hey. I'm not trying to irritate you. Can we talk about it tomorrow?"

I nodded. "But what happened to you isn't an *unfortunate mishap*. They could've killed you. You might not have survived the night on the side of the road. What if it had rained longer and the water rose? It was cold last night. You could've gotten hypothermia."

"I got played, and I got hurt. Pressing charges might get me killed, and I'm partial to living. Those pecan praline doughnuts are reason enough."

My stomach knotted at the thought of something worse happening to him.

"When you can chew without pain, I'll make a batch of doughnuts for you."

"Are you going to sleep?" He shifted his head on the stack of pillows.

"I'm going to try." I carried the dishes into the kitchen and made sure the front door was locked and bolted before going back into the bedroom.

Garrett was already asleep.

Before getting into bed, I took a fast shower. It felt wonderful to be free of mud.

Then I crawled onto the bed and curled up on my side. Watching the rise and fall of his chest, I lay there until my timer went off. Then I returned the peas to the freezer, lay back down, and stopped fighting sleep.

* * *

POUNDING WOKE ME, and I pried my eyes open.

After a frightening second, I remembered why there was a man without a shirt in my bed. I rubbed my face as I rolled off the mattress.

"You were out pretty hard. Your phone buzzed several times." Garrett hooked his thumb toward the doorway. "I can talk to Eli if that will make things easier for you."

"Maybe. I don't know. I thought you didn't want Eli to know." I trudged down the hall, wishing I'd checked the time. I pulled open the door barely an inch. "Hello?"

Eli's green eyes were filled with a wild panic. "What's wrong?"

"Nothing. I was asleep."

"The shop is closed!" He placed a hand on the door, expecting me to swing it open.

I wedged my foot, making sure the door didn't open any farther. "I know. I put the sign up. Can't a woman take a vacation?"

"Not you. You don't know how. That shop has been open every day for seven years. The last time you taped a sign to the door and disappeared was—"

"Don't say it. I'm fine. And I haven't disappeared. I stayed home. Sorry you didn't get coffee." If I talked to Eli much longer, I'd end up telling him all about Garrett's injuries.

"I know you, Tessa. Something is going on." He checked his phone. "But I don't have time to pry the secrets out of you right now. I have to get to work. Call Delaney. She's worried about you."

I nodded before closing the door. Why hadn't I just explained to Eli what was going on?

Two reasons. Garrett didn't want anyone to know, and Eli was too close to Joji, who lived right by Beau Henry's ranch. And she was married to the ranch foreman. The fewer people who knew about Garrett's injuries, the better the chance we had of keeping the fiasco a secret for a week.

Why was I set on protecting Garrett's secret? That was harder to answer.

I shuffled back to the bedroom. "Sorry he woke you up."

"I've been awake. Watching you sleep is more relaxing than actually sleeping right now." He patted the bed. "Tessa, why are you helping me? I hate that I'm putting you in an awkward situation."

Hugging a pillow, I sat down beside him. "When I was twelve, my dad had a garden. He was growing heirloom tomatoes. One day, I heard him fire that stupid BB gun. I ran out back and found an injured squirrel. Dad had just left the poor thing in the yard. He didn't realize he'd wounded it. He was just trying to scare it out of the tomatoes."

"The tomato thief?" Garrett rested his brace next to my hand, and only his thumb was touching me.

"Yeah. That squirrel was eating Dad's prize tomatoes. Anyway, I bandaged the little beast and took him to Eli's house. I spent more time over there than I did at my own house. His mom helped me set up a little bed and feeding station in the garden shed, and I spent a few weeks feeding the little critter and changing the bandages while he healed. When he seemed back to normal, I set him free."

"So I'm a squirrel?" His voice held a hint of humor.

I shrugged. "You need me. At the end of the week, you won't anymore."

"What seemed like a big deal—interrupting the honeymoon—doesn't sound so horrible now. You can't stay closed all week just to take care of me." He shifted toward the edge of the bed. "Besides, if I fall off the radar for too long, folks at the ranch will worry." He sounded so sure, but his shoulders told a different story. His slouch signaled resignation and sadness.

"Where are you going?"

"Take me to get my truck. My phone is in it." He swung one leg over the edge.

I crawled across the bed and grabbed his arm. "No. You aren't giving the orders. *I am*. Get back in this bed."

His muscles flexed under my hand as he obeyed. "Then you need to call Ava."

I didn't want to talk to Ava. She went to church with me. How could I lie to her?

"I really need to find you different clothes." I pulled the sheet back over him.

"I thought you liked looking at my chest."

Dumbfounded by his audacity, I stayed quiet half a second. "I don't..." Trying to lie wasn't going to convince anyone. "I don't want to talk about it."

Garrett laughed and then groaned. "That hurt."

"Serves you right. The bruising is getting worse. Boots?"

He nodded.

"Where's it parked? I'll get your phone and make sure your truck is safe." I kept my back to him, feeling the heat in my cheeks and not wanting him to see me flushed.

"If you don't mind going out to the ranch again, you can get more clothes and my laptop. And if you could let Ava or Clint know that I'm okay, that would be helpful. I'm not sure my voice would be convincing right now."

It was hard to imagine him using a laptop in his condition, but I'd grab it. Maybe his hands weren't broken, just banged up. Badly. Grabbing jeans had been a horrible idea, but I'd been sleep deprived. This time, I'd grab him some sweatpants, some with a drawstring so that they wouldn't ride low on his waist.

"Okay. I'll pick up your prescription while I'm out." I tried to think about what I needed to leave accessible for him. "I'll put some water by the bed and the bag of frozen peas. Will you be okay for a while?"

"Yeah." He told me where to find his truck.

"We can't leave it there."

He lifted his braced and bandaged hands. "I don't have much choice."

"I can get a ride to your truck, then drive it to your cabin." I would have to figure out how to get back home, but I'd think of something.

"And then everyone would wonder about me when I didn't show up for meals. And they'd come knocking, and I wouldn't answer."

I let my hair down, then twisted it back up into a knot and wrapped a scrunchie around it. "Okay, so that doesn't work. I could park it here. But someone might recognize it. I guess that doesn't matter." Someone seeing his car in my lot wouldn't be a big deal. Right? "What should I tell Ava when I go get your clothes?"

Garrett shrugged. "Something that's true. She won't believe you otherwise."

"Yeah. Great. I'll figure something out. And we have to schedule your appointment to get your hands checked. I don't know how I'm going to sneak you out of here."

He rubbed his brace on a wrinkle in the sheet. "Are you planning to keep the shop closed all week?"

"Yes. And it's my choice, so I don't want any pushback." I sat on the edge of the bed. "People can live without dough-nuts for a week. They'll be unhappy but probably thinner."

"I have a suggestion, but you might not like the idea." He still wouldn't look at me.

"Okay?"

"Your sign says you're on vacation, right?" He glanced up but only for a second. "What if I got us a vacation rental in San Antonio? They have places all over the city."

There were benefits to this idea. I wouldn't constantly run into people I knew and have to worry about what I should or shouldn't say. But renting a place with him sounded dangerously close to a relationship, and I was not on board with that.

"I can get us a two-bedroom, so it would be easier than

your place. Then I wouldn't feel guilty about taking up so much of your bed."

That subtle reminder that I'd shared a bed with him had me liking the idea of renting a place with more than one bed. My couch wasn't all that comfortable.

"Think you can find a place for tonight?"

"Possibly."

I laid my laptop on the bed. "If you can get around using your thumb, have at it. If not, I'll find us a place when I get back. Then we can sneak you out when it's dark." I dragged my hands over my face.

"Tessa." Blue eyes focused on me.

"What, Garrett?"

"Don't ever become a spy."

My own laughter surprised me. "Thanks for the tip." I straightened his sheets. Again. "No one has a key, so you won't have anyone popping in to check on me. If they knock, ignore it. I'll be back as soon as I can. And don't forget to ice your hand."

"Yes, ma'am."

I made sure he was comfortable, then headed out before I fussed over him some more.

CHAPTER 4

*R*ide shares into San Antonio were expensive, but I didn't have much of a choice. Since I knew the general area of Garrett's truck, I had the driver drop me off at a mall entrance. The parking lots surrounding the outdoor mall were huge, but how hard could it be to find a vehicle?

Garrett had given detailed instructions about what store he'd parked near and what could be seen from the lot. He'd also mentioned that the lot was nearly empty when he'd parked. That tidbit of info wasn't helpful now.

Looking around to get my bearings, I spotted the roller coaster at the amusement park next to the mall.

I clicked the fob and listened for the beep of the alarm. Only screams from the roller coaster and the low hum of city noises could be heard. Trekking down one row, I scanned for a black truck. Why couldn't he own a red truck or, even better, a yellow one? Those colors would stand out more.

Maybe finding a truck wasn't as easy as I'd first assumed. Was it possible to run a battery down by clicking the remote?

I marched down another row, thankful it wasn't August. The cool November air made this tolerable.

In two rows, I hadn't passed one empty space. Because it was the day after Thanksgiving, thousands of people had opted to go to the mall.

When a car slowed down and started following me through the lot, it wasn't hard to figure out what they wanted —my spot. I just had to find the truck first.

Taillights flashed up ahead, and I ran to the black truck. One item on my list was taken care of. Next up, I needed to get his meds. Saving the most awkward task for last wasn't accidental. I still hadn't figured out what to say to Ava. While I didn't want her to worry, I had to tell her something true. And knocking on her door to tell her Garrett was alive was a horrible way to not raise alarms.

Something would come to me. Hopefully.

After picking up meds and a quick run through the grocery store, I headed out to the ranch. No one was in sight when I parked in front of the cabin, and I sighed. Maybe this wouldn't be bad at all. I hopped out and walked up to his door, keys jingling as I went.

"Hello!" Ava called out as she walked down the hill.

The neighborhood watch here on the ranch was working. I couldn't even sneak into the man's cabin. In the daylight at least.

Smiling like I wasn't keeping secrets, I waved. "Hi, Ava! How are you?"

"Tessa?" She cocked her head.

"It's me. I was just grabbing some stuff for Garrett. We decided on a little getaway. Just a little vacation... kind of." So far, everything I'd said was true.

Her eyebrows lifted. "You and Garrett? I didn't realize..."

"We aren't sleeping together. Separate bedrooms. Because we aren't... I mean... he just..." I needed to shut my mouth. "He seems really nice."

"This explains why you were here last night." Laughter bubbled out of Ava. "Y'all have fun."

What? She knew.

"No. I just came last night to get him some... clothes." My words were not making anything better.

Ava stared at me for a second, her expression serious. "If you and Garrett want to keep your relationship a secret, I can do that. And I'll tell Goldie"—Ava pointed at the first cabin—"not to say anything about you being out here. Call if you need anything."

"Thank you." I ducked into his cabin before she asked me any other questions or before I stated other truths that didn't need to be said. Announcing that we weren't sleeping together probably made it seem like we were. Even if Ava believed that part, now she thought Garrett and I were dating. In secret.

Ugh. Why had I picked up a stranger off the side of the road? Why hadn't I left after he was safely at the hospital?

I knew why I'd picked him up. Leaving an injured man on the side of the road felt wrong. Fear wasn't enough of a reason to leave another person in pain.

The reason I'd stayed with him had everything to do with the way he made me feel, and it scared me a little. I pictured the handsome face and sparkling blue eyes of the man who'd asked me out only weeks ago, and I remembered the tenderness of the pained man who'd wiped tears off my cheek when I wasn't even the one hurting. I couldn't walk away from that. But once he was back on the ranch and had all the help he needed, leaving would be easy.

Glancing around the small cabin, I was somewhat surprised. Beau Henry had money. That was no secret. But Garrett wasn't living like the son of a rich man. This place was smaller than my apartment. And my apartment wasn't big. Nothing had changed since last night, but I'd slept and could now actually process thoughts.

I pulled a duffel bag out of the closet and dug through drawers. I grabbed a clean pair of jeans. Sweatpants would be more comfortable while he healed, and I found two pair in another drawer.

After grabbing a few other items, I took inventory. Shirts, pants, socks, a jacket, tennis shoes. What else did I need to grab? Bathroom stuff. There was a small travel bag in the bathroom drawer, and I threw in the electric shaver and other toiletries. He probably wouldn't be shaving anytime soon, which wasn't a bad thing because he looked pretty good with scruff.

I gave the room one more sweeping glance and thought of showers. If I had to help the man shower, he'd need a swimsuit.

I dug through the drawers until I found two, then shoved them in the bag.

Hovering in the bedroom doorway, I knew I was forgetting something important. But what?

The image of Garrett in that hospital bed was pretty much seared on my brain, and I thought back to what I'd said when he wanted to leave the hospital before I'd grabbed him clothes. "Whatever's under that sheet." Underwear. I hadn't packed any of that. Underwear was important.

After shoving boxer briefs into the bag, I peeked out the kitchen window to make sure Ava wasn't taking a stroll near the cabins, or Goldie for that matter. I'd already said too much. When I was satisfied that the coast was clear, I ran out, hopped in the truck, and zoomed back to the apartment.

Maybe Garrett had booked a place. I hoped so. It would mean a lot less sneaking around. I was tired of sneaking.

* * *

BEFORE I LET myself get distracted by where we'd be staying, I put away groceries, helped Garrett make the appointment to get his hands checked by a specialist, and started a soup.

While it simmered, I went back to the bedroom. "Okay. I think everything is covered. Lunch will be ready in just a few minutes."

"You've been buzzing around since you got home. How did it go at the ranch?"

I chewed my bottom lip and remembered that I'd meant to get more Chapstick. "Um, well... Ava doesn't know that you were hurt, but I'm pretty sure she thinks we're dating."

A smile spread across Garrett's face as he reached for a pillow.

"And it's possible she thinks we're sleeping together."

He hugged the pillow to his chest. "Laughing isn't comfortable."

"Laughing? It isn't funny if she thinks that. But she might've believed me. I told her we weren't sleeping together and that we were getting separate bedrooms on our getaway."

His shoulders bounced as he groaned, his face twisted in pain. "I'm sorry for laughing. I just keep imagining you telling Ava that we aren't sleeping together."

"We aren't!" I wanted to whap him with that pillow.

"I know. It's just that usually makes people think the opposite."

I sat on the edge of the bed. "I was afraid of that, but I hope not because Ava and I go to church together, and her husband used to be the pastor."

Garrett rubbed his bandaged hand on my back. "I'm sorry, Tessa. I shouldn't have asked you to stay at the hospital."

I didn't want to think about that. "And you were wrong

about nobody noticing me in the middle of the night. Ava knew I'd been to your cabin. I don't know how—maybe because of Goldie—so I told her I was there to get your clothes."

He pinched his lips together. "Sorry."

"Did you find a place for us to stay?"

He nodded. "If you open the laptop, I can show you pictures."

"Just tell me about it."

His hand continued to move up and down on my back. "It's a house at the northwest edge of town. There is a kitchen if you want to cook. But I'm not saying you have to. We can order out all week if you prefer. And there's a hot tub."

"Okay. Let me know what I owe you for my half. I need to check the soup." I stopped when I reached the doorway. "Want to eat in here or in the living room?"

"This week is on me. All of it." He swung his legs over the side of the bed. "I'll go out to the living room. Did you get my clothes?"

"Yes. Sorry. They are in the truck. I brought in the groceries and forgot the bag. I gave you your medicine, right?"

He nodded. "Get the bag after we eat. If you can stand looking at my chest a little longer."

"I'll live." I walked back to the bed and helped him up. "Maybe."

He draped an arm around my shoulders, and I pretended that it was because he wanted help down the hall. "If I'd known all it would take to spend a little time with you was to get beaten to a pulp, I might've tried it sooner."

"Funny." I looked up at him and immediately fixed my gaze in front of me. Now that the swelling on his face was going down and his blue eyes were visible, looking him in the eye was more dangerous. Way more dangerous.

Not only had I sworn never to risk picking up another stranger, but I'd also promised my heart I'd never risk it again. Being jilted right before my wedding had been horrible, and I'd sworn I'd never risk falling in love again. Not dating made it easy to keep that promise to myself. This helpless hunk was the first one who'd even made me question that promise.

* * *

I CARRIED Garrett's duffel bag down the hall, nervous at the thought of changing the man's clothes. Without looking at him, I set the bag on the bed and pulled out a pair of sweatpants, boxer briefs, and some socks. "I grabbed T-shirts and a few that button up the front because I wasn't sure how your shoulder was feeling."

"The T-shirt would be more comfortable, but I'll need help getting it on."

Nodding, I chose a super soft shirt. "All right. So..." I inhaled. "First you have to take those clothes off."

"This is a bit awkward, but if you'll unbutton my pants, I can handle the rest." He held up his hands, showing that he'd worked his thumb loose from the bandage. "The doctor said the bandages could come off tonight anyway."

"He said they needed to be changed tonight. Not exactly the same thing." Standing in front of Garrett, I unfastened the button, then squeezed my eyes closed as I lowered the zipper. "All good?"

"Thanks."

With my eyes still closed, I spun around. "I'm not looking."

Change rattled in a pocket as his jeans hit the floor, and I slapped a hand over my eyes, knowing what was coming off next.

The mattress shifted, and Garrett's breathing sped up.

I inched away from the bed.

A loud thunk sounded behind me, and Garrett grunted.

If he'd broken something else, this was going to be way more complicated.

"Do you—"

"Don't turn around. I'm okay." His voice was strained, and he didn't sound all that okay.

As one minute stretched into two, he shifted and grunted, but I kept my eyes covered. After what seemed like forever, he stilled. "I'm really sorry. I tried to get dressed, but I'm going to need help with the pants. My boxer briefs are on. I managed that."

"Sure. Yeah." This was no big deal. Just because I'd never seen a man in his underwear—not true. I'd seen one, but I'd blocked out that memory. But this wasn't weird. Not at all. I'd seen guys in swimsuits. It was almost the same thing. Shoot. Boxer briefs covered more than some swimsuits. I forced a smile as I turned around.

Garrett was on the floor, a sheepish look on his face. "Help. I've fallen, and I can't get up."

I tried not to look directly at him, but that lasted all of a millisecond. "Garrett, your legs. They are covered in bruises."

"I'm one big bruise right now. And it feels like it."

If I focused too long on his injuries, I'd start crying, and that would be embarrassing since I wasn't the one hurt. "Do you want pants first, or should we get you off the floor before we deal with the pants?"

"It'll probably be easier to get pants on once I'm back on the bed."

"All right. We've done this once already. We can do it

again. We'll just try to skip the part where I fall over and end up with you on top of me." I tried to remember how I'd gotten him up the last time.

"Is there a raincheck available for that?"

I rolled my eyes. "Okay. Now that I know your ribs are hurt, grabbing you around the chest doesn't seem like such a great idea."

He bent his knees. "If I can get on all fours, I can use the bed to get up." After rolling onto his side, he shifted a leg.

I hovered over him, not sure where to touch to help him. "What do you need me to do?"

"If you could shove my hips up, that would help. With my abs sore and limited use of my hands, getting into position is difficult."

With my hands on his hips, I helped him onto his knees. "What now?"

Braced on his elbows, he looked up at the bed. "I just need to reach the edge of the bed."

"And I would love to have a gourmet kitchen." I needed something for him to use to push up a little. "Okay. I have a plan. I dropped to my knees and crawled between Garrett and the bed. "Use my back to get up."

"I owe you, Tessa. Seriously." He managed to get upright enough to get his feet underneath him. Then he sat down on the bed. "After this week, will you even speak to me?"

"Not sure yet. But don't be surprised if I always look near you and not directly at you." I helped him get his feet onto the bed.

"If you can get the waistband up to at least my knees, I can do the rest."

"Without falling off the bed?"

His blue eyes twinkled. "Maybe."

He wriggled into his pants without much of a problem.

Putting on his shirt should've been the easiest part. But it wasn't, because the temptation to press soft kisses to each of his bruises pounded on the inside of my skull. Kissing him was the opposite of not risking my heart.

I recognized it for what it was. Physical attraction. Nothing more.

CHAPTER 5

Following the directions on my map app, I drove through a very upscale neighborhood. "What kind of place did you get?"

"Someplace where we wouldn't be bothered." He grinned as the voice on my phone instructed me to turn into a driveway. "And I wanted it to be worth closing your shop. I'll hide out, and you can enjoy a mini vacation."

The driveway wound through trees before circling in front of a massive two-story house. Just before the house, the driveway branched off toward a garage.

I stopped and gazed up at the house through the windshield. "Garrett, this is huge."

"It looks nice."

"Wow. Yeah. Nice. We'll go with that. I'll get you unloaded here, then park in the garage, I guess." After unbuckling my seat belt, I leaned over and clicked the button on his. "This definitely qualifies as a getaway."

He climbed out of the car on his own as I yanked bags out of the backseat. "Sorry I can't help you with those. I feel like a heel, letting you do all the work."

"Not a big deal. They aren't heavy."

"I ordered some stuff earlier. It should be delivered some-time in the next hour." Garrett stepped onto the porch, then dictated the code for me to punch into the key box.

I unlocked the door and pushed it open. Momentarily forgetting the bags, I walked inside in awe. On the other side of a large living room was a wall of floor-to-ceiling windows and a set of double doors that led out to a huge deck. I stepped outside. The house had been built onto a hill, and the view from here was breathtaking. Lights twinkled on the horizon. Down the hill and to the left and right, windows of large houses glowed. But even the view of those houses was obscured by trees. How could a house in the city feel so private?

Farther down the deck was another set of double doors and close to them was a hot tub. Lounge chairs dotted the deck near there and on the other side was a table with a fire pit in the middle. Beside it was an outdoor sofa and chairs.

I whipped around and planted my hands on Garrett's chest, which thankfully now had a shirt covering it. "Sorry. I didn't realize you were behind me."

"Do you like it, Tessa?"

Nodding, I smiled up at him. "I do. And if it didn't cause you excruciating pain, I'd hug you."

"Can I get a raincheck on that too?"

"Sure." I followed him back inside. "Oh my stars! Look at the kitchen!" I loved to cook and bake, and this kitchen was a dream. "I'm definitely cooking this week."

"Whatever you want. We can order more groceries tomorrow if needed."

"I brought some with me. Speaking of which, I need to bring our stuff inside." I rubbed his back. "This place is amazing."

I rushed out to get the stuff, thinking about how fun it

would be to call Delaney and gush about this place, but how would I explain being here? I needed to figure something out because as soon as Ava talked to Delaney, it wouldn't be a secret that I was here with Garrett.

"Okay. I want to explore the rest of the house, but I really need to call Delaney. She's probably worried, and then she'll get Eli worried. That would be bad. I'm just going to tell them I'm with you."

"I like the sound of that." One side of his mouth twitched up.

"One week. It's not like I'm pretending we're a couple or anything. We—I mean *you*—rented this amazing house, and we are staying here for a few days." I buried my face in my hands. "It totally sounds like we're dating."

"Not to me." He eased himself down to the couch. "Go call Delaney."

I pressed her name in my contacts as I stepped out to the porch.

Delaney answered after one ring. "Tessa! Hey. Let's switch to video. I want to make sure you're okay."

"I'm fine. Look where I am. It's incredible." I switched to video and showed her the view from the deck. "This is where I'm vacationing. Garrett rented a place on the edge of San Antonio, and I'm staying with him here." I kept talking even though her jaw hung open. "I haven't even walked through the entire house yet. There are like five bedrooms and a to-die-for kitchen. Did I mention the hot tub?"

"You and Garrett? Beau's son?"

"Yeah. He's a nice guy." I kept the camera pointed out toward the view.

Delaney huffed. "I want to see your face."

I switched the camera. "What?"

"You're telling the truth. Why did I not know you were dating Garrett?" She sounded almost hurt.

47

"No one said anything about dating. We're just spending a week together."

She stared at me. "There is something you aren't telling me. You have told me multiple times that you don't date. And now you are spending a week with Garrett?"

"It's just a week. I'm not dating him." Just a week was going to be my new mantra.

"Put Garrett on the phone. I want to talk to him."

"No!" I glanced back toward the house, making sure he was out of view. "You know Garrett?"

"Yes. He and Eli are friends." She said it so matter-of-factly.

"Eli mentioned that. Not that you'd met Garrett. Just that they were friends." I sat down on the outdoor sofa and pulled my jacket closed.

Delaney rolled her eyes. "I tried to get him to set you up with Garrett. But Eli said that ever since Mosquito Boy—"

"Skeeter."

Her nose crinkled. "Was that his real name?"

"No, but I liked that better than Cornelius." Seven years seemed like a lifetime ago.

"Anyway, Eli said you haven't dated since that jerk cheated on you and called off the wedding. And for the record, Eli called him Mosquito Boy."

"Yeah. Eli wasn't a fan. And he was right. And, just so you know, Eli offered to set me up with Garrett if I changed my mind about dating." I covered a yawn. "I should go. Garrett's waiting on me."

Eli just hadn't used Garrett's name. He offered to set me up with the guy from the doughnut shop, and the fact that I instantly knew who he'd meant only fueled Eli's matchmaking attempt.

"I know you're keeping secrets." Delaney's words sliced through my thoughts.

48

I chewed my lip, trying to figure out how to respond. "Please don't ask me any questions. I'm okay, and I'll be home in a week."

Delaney stared at the screen, then after a couple of heartbeats, she nodded. "Keep in touch, please. And I'm so glad you finally took a vacation. You work too much."

"All right. Bye." I ended the call before she changed her mind about grilling me.

Why did she have to bring up Skeeter? Now I'd be comparing Garrett to the toad all week, and I knew how that scorecard would look. Even all beat up, Garrett was better looking. But I'd also be remembering what Skeeter said. Maybe remembering wasn't such a bad thing.

I trudged back inside. "Want to tour the rest of the house?"

"Yeah. At least this floor." He glanced at the stairs. "I might save the stairs for tomorrow."

We walked into the master bedroom, the room with doors that opened to the patio and hot tub. I'd never seen a bed as large as the one dominating this room. "What kind of bed is that? It's huge."

"The write-up mentioned that one master had an Alaskan King, and the other master on this floor had a Texas King. I guess those are bigger than regular king-sized beds." He walked into the bathroom. "It has a walk-in shower. That's good."

"The other master must be over here across the hall." I stepped into the other room, which was equally as large and had a balcony on the side of the house. I sat on the bed, bouncing a little. This place was nicer than any place I'd ever stayed.

Garrett poked his head into the room. "Someone knocked. They'll need to see your ID because I ordered wine."

I hurried to the door, digging my ID out of my bag. "Hi."

The delivery guy held up an armload of bags. "Should I put these on the counter?"

"Please." I moved out of the way as he carried in the haul.

After putting the bags down, he checked my ID. "Thank you, Miss Best. I hope you and your boyfriend have a nice night."

I whipped around to see Garrett leaning against the far wall in the living room. "He's not my boyfriend."

"If you say so." The delivery guy looked from me to Garrett, then shrugged before slipping out the door.

It closed with a bang.

"What did you order? And there is no way I'm letting you have wine. It doesn't mix well with pain meds." I unloaded the bags and breathed in deep when I felt Garrett walk up behind me.

"The wine was for you. I hope you like what I bought. And I'm sorry, Tessa. You'll probably never see him again. It doesn't matter what he thinks." Garrett leaned around to look me in the face. "I know we aren't dating, and you know we aren't dating. That's all that matters."

"Right." I went back to unloading. "I'll get dinner started. Then we can figure out something to do."

"We could make use of that huge television in the master bedroom and watch a movie."

"Sounds good."

* * *

BIRDS CHIRPED, and I kept my eyes closed, content with my dream. Snuggled against a faceless person, I relaxed as his heart repeated a ker-thump. The warmth felt so real that I almost kicked off my blanket.

I needed to wake up. Garrett would need breakfast and more pain meds.

Before giving up my dream, I sighed, and my dream man responded by hugging me closer.

But when I opened my eyes, the heartbeat and the warmth didn't go away.

"You fell asleep before the movie ended." Garrett's voice was soft and tender.

I sat up and rubbed sleep out of my eyes. "Sorry. After they stole that car, I just…" Then I glanced at the other side of the bed, where an entire four feet or more appeared untouched.

He chuckled. "That's what they did through the whole movie—they stole cars."

"I didn't mean to cuddle you. I hope I didn't hurt you." I crawled to the far edge of the bed. "You must be hungry."

"Tessa." Concern added an edge to his voice.

Shaking my head, I walked out to the living room. I could put distance between us, but I couldn't forget how good it felt to be snuggled against him. It wasn't his tall, muscly build or those amazing blue eyes that had me thinking about him all the time. It was the way he said my name, the tender gestures from a man who tried to be strong even when he wasn't, and his vulnerability.

But that vulnerability would go away when he'd healed and was no longer dependent on me for food and clean clothes. Even if it didn't go away, there was no way I could be vulnerable in return.

CHAPTER 6

*a*fter feeding Garrett breakfast and only speaking when spoken to, I unwrapped his hand. "The scrapes still look bad. After the shower, we'll put on fresh bandages. Did they say if anything was broken in this hand?"

"Honestly. I don't remember. But based on the condition of the outside of my hand, I'm guessing the inside isn't in great shape. But I hate not being able to use my hands." He wiggled his fingers on the other hand and winced. "The doctor said I could take the brace off to shower."

"But then it goes right back on after we ice it. I laid out clothes on the bed. And once you're decent, I'll come in and help with the rest." I wiped down the counter. Again.

"How many times are you going to clean that spot?"

Until I stopped thinking about being snuggled against your chest. Thankfully, I didn't say that out loud. "There was a crumb. Do you need me to do anything else?"

"Tell me why things are so different this morning. I swear nothing happened last night. When it got cold in the house, you cuddled next to me, and I put my arm around you. That's it." He laid his battered hand on mine. "Please tell me what's bothering you."

"After your shower. Maybe. I'm going to prep lunch; then we can play a game or..." I shrugged.

"Enjoy the hot tub. I can leave my bandages off just a little longer."

The hot tub sounded so relaxing. "Okay. I'll lay out your swimsuit."

He followed me into the bedroom but kept his distance. I appreciated that, but a small part of me hated not having him near me. Stupid attraction.

I pulled out one of his swimsuits. "You want it on the bed?"

"Sure. Just—you know—close the door on your way out." All the tease was gone from his blue eyes.

I laughed, hoping to lighten the mood. "Yeah. I won't come in unless you yell my name. No matter how loud a thud."

"Deal."

In the kitchen, I rummaged through the cabinets, finding what I'd need to make doughnuts. Thankfully, this house was well-stocked, and I'd brought all the groceries I needed. Garrett's mouth pain seemed to be easing, so today's snack would be doughnuts. His favorite flavor. I'd make the dough while he showered and let it rise while we soaked in the hot tub.

I still doubted the wisdom of saying yes to his suggestion, but the warmth of the hot tub could make it easier to talk about why waking up next to him bothered me. I just needed to figure out what to say. "It's not you. It's me" was not the right way to start the conversation. But at the end of the day, that was the truth. Someone as amazing as Garrett deserved someone equally as incredible. That person wasn't me.

Thinking about it made my chest tight, so I put it off for now. I'd think about what to say later. Or wing it.

After opening cabinets and looking through the pantry, I was amazed. I couldn't even imagine how much he had to be paying per night for this place. They had everything. Finding a standup mixer in the pantry was both unexpected and wonderful. My arms would be grateful.

I warmed the milk and mixed it with sugar and yeast, then let it sit for a few minutes.

While the yeast did its thing, I checked my messages.

Delaney had texted: *Anything exciting?*

Instead of texting her back, I called. The shower was still going, so I figured I'd have a few minutes of privacy.

Delaney answered right away. "Hey there. Talk to me."

"I need to get back to making the dough in a few minutes, but I thought I'd call. I'm good."

"Dough? Are you making doughnuts?"

"Garrett likes the praline pecan kind." And now I was making his favorite things. Every time I talked to Delaney, it started to sound more like Garrett and I were dating.

"And you aren't good. I can tell that from your voice. What's wrong?"

"He's sweet and kind and… warm." I closed my eyes, falling right back into the dream. "He's so many things I wish I'd waited for the first time I gave my heart away. But I can't do it again. I was a complete mess. It wasn't pretty." I'd said way more to her than I'd intended.

"You graciously pointed out my flaws when I needed to hear the truth, so take this advice in that same vein. You aren't the same person who was engaged to Skeeter. And giving Garrett a *tiny* chance doesn't mean you are headed down the same path as before."

"I'm not sure I'm capable of giving him a *tiny* chance. I either need to toss my heart in the deep freeze to keep it protected or lay it out to be butchered. Those are the choices." I also hadn't told Delaney everything, and I wasn't about to change that now.

"That is the worst imagery for love I've ever heard."

"No one said *anything* about love." The door opened at the end of the hall. "Gotta go." I smiled at the bubbles in the mixing bowl, hoping Garrett wouldn't notice how flustered I was. "That was a quick shower."

Water droplets clung to Garrett's brown hair. A few fell onto his chest and cut a path downward across his bruised abs. After watching two drops race toward his waistband, I went back to mixing ingredients.

"I didn't want you to worry about me and forget the deal. Especially after I dropped the shampoo bottle." He rested his folded arms on the counter. "I feel almost human."

"I didn't even hear it fall. I'm so sorry. Next time, I'll stay closer."

"We'll figure it out. What are you making?"

I turned on the mixer and let it go for a minute before adding the rest of the flour. "Your favorite. They won't be ready for a while. The dough has to rise for more than an hour."

"I can't wait."

"Remind me when we get out of the hot tub to rub that cream on your bruises. It will help them heal faster." I pulled the bag of frozen peas out, wrapped it in a kitchen towel, and slid it across the counter. "Hold that against your face while I finish the dough."

"Yes, ma'am." He held it against his face. "Seeing myself in the mirror was a bit of a shock. I look pretty bad."

"Just a few cuts and bruises. You'll heal." I liked his face even when it turned funny colors and looked like he'd been pumped full of air. "I can see your eyes now. That's nice. The swelling went down pretty quick."

"The guy never hit me directly in the eye, so they thought the swelling was from an allergy of some sort. Or insect bites. I laid in the grass for hours, so who knows?" He was talking more about the incident, but he still hadn't told me everything.

"Well, it's nice to see your eyes again."

"If I tell you that I think you're beautiful, will you quit talking to me?" He still had the frozen bag covering his face.

"Probably."

"Then I won't say it." He set the bag down.

I motioned for him to pick up the bag. "It hasn't been twenty minutes. Put it back on your face. It helps with the swelling."

"You said the swelling had gone down."

"On your eyes. But that spot on your cheek still looks bad."

He complied with my wishes. "Did you study to be a nurse?"

"No. I just know how to search on Google. Speaking of which, the next time we order groceries, get pineapple or pineapple juice." I transferred the dough to an oiled bowl and covered it with a towel. "I'm going to turn the heat up a little in the house. It will help the dough, and we won't be so cold when we come back in from the hot tub."

Garrett blinked and pulled the frozen peas away from his face. "You want me to eat pineapple?"

"Is that so weird? You aren't allergic, are you?"

"No. I just…" He scratched his head as he walked away from the counter, then turned back around. "Why pineapple?"

"Because it has some enzyme in it that fights pain and is an anti-inflammatory. Why are you acting like pineapple is weird?"

He shook his head. "Turning up the heat is a good plan."

But the hot tub wasn't a good plan. I could feel how bad the idea was all the way to my toes. But the other thing I felt all the way to my toes was attraction. I blamed it on his lack of shirt.

"Let me change into my swimsuit and grab us some towels." I hurried back to the bedroom.

"I'll meet you out by the hot tub."

* * *

THE FLUFFY ROBE I'd found hanging in the bathroom helped keep the cold at bay as I tiptoed out to the hot tub. Garrett had said he'd meet me out there, but I didn't realize he meant in the hot tub.

I tossed my robe over the back of a chair. "Why did you get in by yourself? You could've slipped."

He kept his back to me, his head leaning on the ledge and his eyes closed. "Swimsuit fell off, and it was easier to just get in rather than wrestle that thing back on with my thumbs."

I yanked my foot out of the water. I couldn't get into the hot tub with him when he was... not dressed. I shivered as my brain struggled to think of an excuse. And the bubbles made it hard to see below the surface of the water.

Scanning the ground, I tried to spot his swimsuit. How far had he walked without it on? "Oh. I, um... I think I'm going to go back in and..."

"Watch dough rise? Tessa, I was..." He turned around, and his unfinished sentence hung in the air as his gaze traveled from my head to my toes. The moment of silence was brief but obvious. "I was joking. I have a swimsuit on."

"Okay." Easing into the water, I sighed at how good the warm bubbles felt after standing in the cold. "Sometimes, I have a hard time knowing if you're serious or not."

"I've gathered that. And it's kind of fun." He eyed me as I moved toward him.

My plan was to sit beside him. Not too close. But the strands of hair hanging into his face were going to bug me. I stood in front of him and combed my fingers through his brown hair. "Sorry I didn't offer to help you comb it. I didn't think about how hard it was for you to hold a comb."

Garrett stayed quiet as I smoothed down the parts that were sticking up and pushed a few strands away from his eyes.

"I like your hair this length. It has a nice wave to it. I bet the ends start to curl when it gets longer."

He rested his hands on my hips, and I slid my hands out of his hair and pressed them to his chest, ready to push away.

"Tessa, if any other woman played with my hair like that —especially in a hot tub—I'd assume she was flirting. And if I were attracted to her, I'd respond with a long passionate kiss that would make her toes pop off. And maybe make my toes pop off too."

I wiggled my toes, staring at the bubbles dancing on the surface. Because he was sitting and I was standing, we were almost eye to eye. I didn't pull away.

"But in the few days that we've been *compadres*, I don't think you've intentionally flirted once. Shoot, I'm not even sure if you like me. You might not."

I shook my head because I didn't want him thinking I didn't like him, but all the words I wanted to say were tangled in a lump in my throat.

"And it's okay if you aren't attracted to me. I can live with that. I've been turned down by beautiful—sorry, I won't call you that—by women before, and I'll deal. We can be friends, though, and have a great time this week."

Nodding, I didn't say anything because I didn't trust my voice. But I loved the idea of being Garrett's friend.

"And just so we're clear on a few things. I'm not asking out a different woman every weekend. In fact, when I asked you out a few weeks ago, that was the first time I'd asked a woman out since moving to Texas."

"More than a year ago. That's why Ava was so surprised to find me at your cabin." I braved a moment of eye contact.

His head bobbed slightly. "You remind me of Ava, and I mean that as a compliment. She's giving and caring and makes it seem effortless. She can make a person feel welcome with only her smile. I imagine that all those kids at school who bragged about going home to fresh baked cookies had moms who were like Ava."

I knew Ava well enough to appreciate what a compliment it was. "She has a heart of gold."

"You do too."

I didn't want to talk about me. I wasn't ready to drag the skeletons out of my closet and babble about my broken engagement. "How has it been? Finding your dad and starting over in a new place are big life changes."

Garrett turned me around and pulled me into his lap. The move was protective, not of me but of himself. I didn't mind in the least because friends snuggled in the hot tub, right? Maybe he was cold. It was colder than yesterday. The temperatures today hovered near freezing. After deciding that it was fine for friends to sit this close in the hot tub, I relaxed against him.

He responded by wrapping his arms around my waist. "Finding my dad was good for me. I didn't expect him to be a wealthy rancher. Usually, the dads who are never discussed have earned that because of crime or other bad behavior. Beau—Dad—is the exception. But I've gotten more than a dad out of the deal. Lilith is a hoot, and she's a great stepmom. She loves my dad. That's obvious." He shifted his arms a little and stared out at the skyline. "Ava and Clint treat me like one of their own. And they both married great people. It's been fun to see people fall in love on the ranch. Even the ranch hands have been welcoming. I have a family there." He met my gaze. "And there are perks to being Beau Henry's son. I can afford this place because of the rather large account he set up for me. But this is the first time I've actually used that account."

"I heard the stories. You treated them like family even before you knew Beau was your dad." I glanced back at him. "Do you feel guilty about using the money?"

"For this? No."

Between the warmth of the hot tub and not facing each other, this was the perfect place to talk. About him. I wasn't ready to talk about me. "Beau owns a massive ranch, but you aren't working for him. That surprises me."

"The guys who work there have spent years doing that kind of work. I'm not sure how it would go over if I raced in and acted like I wanted to take over the place. I know Dad would love for me to learn how to run the ranch, and I help out from time to time. Throwing hay and other stuff."

"That explains a lot. Both about the muscles and the ranch. I think maybe you are afraid you won't be good at it right away. You're afraid to look like a failure." I probably should've run those words through a filter before saying them out loud, but now they were out in the wild.

"That's scarily accurate. But let's talk about the muscles. Please expand on that."

"I think you'd be good at ranching."

He leaned close, and his breath tickled my ear. "Are you trying to avoid talking about my muscles?"

"No. You have the kind of muscles that look like they've come from hard work and not from the gym." For someone set on not dating, I had strong opinions about muscles.

"Are you saying the guys at the gym don't work hard?"

I shook my head, rubbing my hair against his shoulder. "All I'm saying is that I find your type of muscle more attractive."

"So you think I'm attractive?"

I knew better than to answer that question. "Given your current condition, it seems to me that working on a ranch would be far less dangerous than whatever it is you're doing now." I tilted my head up to see his reaction.

He studied my face before leaning in closer. Garrett was going to kiss me. I sucked in a breath, then licked my lips. Did I want him to? I wasn't sure. The voices in my head couldn't agree on an answer.

He stopped before his lips touched me, and he brushed the tip of his nose on mine. "I'm not going to kiss you, Tessa. I want to. Believe me; I do, but your entire body tensed, which tells me you don't want me to kiss you. Maybe it means you don't want me to kiss you *yet*. I hope so, but I'd never take what wasn't offered. When I kiss you, it will be because you want me to."

That was not the sort of declaration to be left unanswered, but it took me several seconds to find my voice. "Garrett, I—"

A snowflake landed on his nose.

He grinned as he flicked it away.

"It's snowing!" I'd never been more excited about frozen precipitation. It made this sweet intimate moment even more memorable.

Tiny white flakes fell onto the deck and into the hot tub.

"It sure is. This is a rare moment."

"Right? It hardly ever snows in these parts. This is amazing." Enjoying the perfect scene, I rested my arms on his and leaned my head back onto his shoulder. "I'm not hurting you, am I?"

His stubble brushed the side of my head as he whispered

in my ear. "You make me feel a lot of things, but pain isn't one of them."

My brain yanked out the scorecard and started marking boxes. Then Skeeter's voice shattered the pretty little snow globe in my head.

CHAPTER 7

*A*fter getting out of the shower, I pulled on leggings and a baggy sweatshirt. Then I tied my hair up in a messy bun before heading to Garrett's room. Not dating meant I didn't have to put on makeup or wear cute clothes. My attire and my lack of makeup embraced the idea of vacation.

I tapped on his door. "You decent?"

"Mostly."

That one word helped me mentally prepare. I needed to rub cream into his bruises so they'd heal quickly, and since his bruises were all over his body, anything more than his boxer briefs would inhibit access to said bruises. So, I expected he was wearing only his underwear. And I was right.

He sat on the edge of the bed. "I waited to put clothes on because you said you had something you needed to do to my bruises."

"You combed your hair."

A nod preceded his smile. "Combing it was only mildly painful."

"You didn't like me touching your hair?" I picked up the tube of arnica cream and squirted a little into my hand.

"Didn't say that. But I might've liked it too much." He rolled his shoulders. "Where do you want me?"

His nervousness ramped up my feelings of awkwardness about rubbing cream all over him. And I couldn't very well do it with my eyes closed. The whole point was to get it on the bruises.

"Let me lay out a towel, then we won't accidentally get anything on the bed." I grabbed one out of the bathroom and spread it out one-handed.

He lay down on his back. "This okay for starters?"

"Perfect." I touched one of the cuts on his lip. "This is healing nicely. Does it still hurt?"

"Not much."

"That means yes, doesn't it?" I gently rubbed cream on the bruised spots on his face. "What happened, Garrett? When I think of someone hitting you hard enough to cause this damage, I ache. It hurts me. Help me understand what happened."

My fingers glided over his muscles. On his chest, there were only a couple of bruises. His abs had more.

Garrett eyed my hands as they moved down his body. "I can't really tell you without explaining what I do, and that would make things complicated for you."

"Seriously, Garrett? You aren't a spy. Don't give me the 'If I told you, I'd have to kill you' bit. Just tell me."

He flexed. Either he was trying to impress me—spoiler, he already had—or he was ticklish. I ignored it and kept working.

"You were adamant about not knowing because it would make things awkward with Delaney. And she needs her best friend's help to plan the wedding. I'm not going to be the reason you can't talk to her or the reason her—" He snapped his head up off the pillow as I rubbed his thigh. "I almost said too much."

I moved down to his lower legs. "Tell me what you do. Forget what I said before." When I finished with the top of him, I tapped his hip. "Roll over."

"I'm a private investigator." He shifted and stretched out on his stomach.

I sucked in a deep breath and fanned myself.

"You okay?" He turned his head and looked up at me.

"Uh-huh." I squeezed more cream into my hand. "Fine. Yeah."

"Tessa, if you want to skip the rest—"

"Oh no. I'll finish up really quick." The private investigator bit made sense, but it still surprised me. "You're kind of like a spy. That's cool." I took another deep breath before rubbing his back. This part of him had gotten the worst of the beating. "Your back is so bruised." I trailed my finger over one of the worst spots.

Garrett stilled.

"I'm sorry for touching you like that. It's just…" I wiped at a tear. "I'm almost done." I rubbed cream on him, like I should have been doing instead of caressing his back.

"Looks bad, huh? Those are mostly from boots. I was curled up on the ground." He reached out and patted my leg. "I didn't mean for you to get upset."

"I'm okay." I finished up my task. "Did you investigate the wrong person? Not that you were tailing the wrong person. I meant… were you investigating someone who wasn't a good person? That question sounds stupid out loud. Of course they weren't a nice person if they did this to you." I tapped his shoulder. "I'm done. Let me run and wash my hands."

I welcomed the small break. Talking had made rubbing the cream on him less awkward this time, but talking about what happened made me want to hug him. I shouldn't want to hug him. But friends hugged.

When I walked back out, he had on his sweatpants and was pulling a shirt over his head. "Hey. Come here." He rested his hands on my hips when I moved in front of him. "A woman hired me to investigate her husband. She wanted proof that he was cheating, and she told me where I could expect to find him."

Anger burned in my chest. "He was a cheater. Figures."

"I don't think he was. I think I got played. He grabbed me seconds after I stepped out of my truck, and when he and his buddy were driving me out to his house, the man ranted about stalking his wife and laying my hands on her."

Being as gentle as I could, I wrapped my arms around him.

He pulled me closer. "I can't blame the man for protecting his wife. I'd be angry too if I thought someone I loved was in danger."

"You wouldn't beat someone to a pulp and leave them on a dark road. On *Thanksgiving*."

"Maybe not. But I was set up. I just can't figure out why." He rested his head on my shoulder. "That's why I didn't press charges."

"I want to hire you."

Garrett pulled back with his eyebrows lifted. "I'm currently not taking new cases."

"Well, when you do, after your hands heal, I want you to investigate something for me. I'll pay your regular rate." I stepped back. "I need to bandage your hand and put the brace back on."

He caught my hand. "That can wait a second. What's the case?"

"Be careful with your hand." I wasn't brave enough to look at him while I spoke, so I focused on his neck where it curved and disappeared under his collar. It was a nice spot, one of only a few without bruises. "Some woman, who I would be perfectly happy leaving on the side of a dark road—that's not true. I'd feel guilty about that—anyway, she hurt someone I care about, a friend, and I want to know why, *and* I want her to get what's coming to her."

Garrett brushed his thumb against my cheek. "That's very sweet."

"She can't get away with this." I looked down at his scraped and bruised hand. "She can't."

His thumb grazed the tops of my knuckles. "Let's get those bandages on so you can make my doughnuts."

"How about some homemade bacon mac and cheese for lunch? I'll make that first, then tackle the doughnuts."

"Sounds good."

I wasn't dense enough not to realize that despite my frequent pep talks I'd developed feelings for Garrett. Which was silly because I'd spent less than forty-eight hours with him. With this realization, my plan changed from trying not to develop feelings—that train had left the station—to not acting on those feelings.

I needed to figure out what was acceptable in the friend zone because I was pretty sure we'd spent most of the morning outside the zone, pretending we were in the zone.

* * *

I ROLLED out the dough and picked up my doughnut cutter. Making him doughnuts had been on my agenda for this week, and I'd come prepared. "Tell me about where you grew up. About your family."

"On one condition."

"You're putting conditions on our friendship?" I grinned as I transferred perfect circles to the tray.

"I want to make sure it's a two-way street." He pulled the bag of peas away from his face for a second. "I want to hear your story next."

"It's nothing exciting, but I'll tell you." Once the tray was full, I tested the oil to make sure it was up to temp. "Are you talking about growing up or… other stuff?"

"Whatever you are willing to share."

I nodded as I dropped the first few doughnuts into the oil. What I was willing to share changed by the minute. Not because of anything Garrett said or did, but because of my level of courage and coherent thought.

He pressed the peas to his face. "I grew up next door to my grandparents. My mom was a little too attached to her family, and that's why I grew up without a dad. But that's a story for another time. For me, living beside my grandparents was a good thing. My grandma was like Ava. After school, I'd go to her house, and she'd have cookies and milk waiting for me. When I was in high school, my mom remarried. After that, I spent countless hours at my grandparents' house or fishing with my granddad. My stepdad wasn't horrible; he just made me feel like I was in the way."

"I'm sorry."

He shrugged. "When I graduated from high school, I left for college and never moved back home. On holidays, I'd stay with my grandparents, which infuriated my mom the first time. I feel a little bad about that now. But I stayed where I felt the most welcome."

I pulled the first batch out of the oil and dipped them in the glaze. "These aren't ready. You have to be patient."

"Yes, ma'am." He chuckled as he poked at the glaze on a doughnut. "Anyway, my stepdad died a year before my mom. My grandparents passed away a few months before that. It was a rough few years."

"How long was it after your mom died until you met

Beau?" I drizzled on the praline icing and added pecans to the top of each doughnut.

"About three months." He tugged the tray toward him. "Have I waited long enough?"

"Dig in." I held my breath as he took a bite.

His moan was a good sign. "Oh, Tessa. This is incredible. I thought they were good before, but warm, they are on a whole different level of good." He nudged the tray toward me. "Aren't you going to have one?"

"I don't eat doughnuts anymore." I rarely admitted that to anyone, but the words just popped out.

"You are an interesting person, Tessa Best." He closed his eyes as he took another bite. "I bet you heard a lot of jokes about your last name."

"Yep. I was the *best* at everything. My ex was one of the worst about that. He always told people I was his *Best* girl. I should've taken the hint. Being his best meant I wasn't his only." I spun around and stuck my head in the fridge, pretending to search for something.

Garrett pretended like I hadn't just dropped a bomb. "I feel your pain. I had similar issues."

"Let me guess. You were always Mr. Right."

"Bingo." He held up his hand and wiggled his thumb and forefinger. "Leaving these unwrapped is really helpful. Good call."

"Now you don't need me to feed you." I had mixed feelings about that.

"But I still need you."

What was I going to do at the end of the week when he didn't need me anymore?

I'd wake up every morning and make the doughnuts just like I'd done for the last seven years.

CHAPTER 8

As soon as the movie ended, I jumped up and stretched. "I'm headed to bed."

Garrett's brow wrinkled. "It's eight thirty."

"Yeah, and by the time I change into my jammies, wash my face, and brush my teeth, it'll be a quarter to nine. Then I'll read for fifteen minutes before turning out the light." I walked into the kitchen and filled a glass with water before getting one of his pills out of the bottle. "Here's your pain pill. I'm guessing these make it easier to sleep."

He shrugged and held out his hand. "It helps." After swallowing his medicine, he stood. "What are you reading?"

"A romance novel."

His low chuckle was as satisfying as a warm doughnut. "That's kind of like you not eating doughnuts. You read about what you won't do, and you make what you won't eat."

That one sentence summed up my entire adult life. But how could he know that?

"What? I never said..." Had I talked in my sleep? At no point during our time together had I mentioned my issues with relationships, other than the slip about Skeeter.

"Let's call it an educated guess on my part. You seriously go lights out at nine? Every night?" He winced as he stretched.

"Okay, Mr. Spy, I get that you live the night life and chase people around in the shadows long after I'm asleep, but the doughnuts don't make themselves. The shop opens at six. And people show up, expecting to get doughnuts, which means I have to make them before six." I picked up my phone. "We lead opposite lives."

That was another good reminder of why I shouldn't risk my heart on Garrett.

After getting ready for bed, I pulled back the covers and slid between the sheets. I wanted to know the thread count because these sheets were the most luxurious fabric I'd ever had against my skin.

I opened the book and tried reading where I'd left off. Normally, I'd be excited about the hero finally kissing the heroine, but tonight, my heart was torn. Reading about what I wouldn't do wasn't entertaining right now, so I closed the book and flopped back on the goose-down pillows.

My brain replayed the day like a movie reel, and when it reached the end, I sat up. It'd been hours since we'd eaten. I probably should've given Garrett a snack with his pill. Taking meds on an empty stomach was a bad idea. He was probably still awake.

Two steps out of my room, I could tell the living room was dark, but his bedroom door was still open.

"Garrett?" I rapped on the open door before walking in. "You awake?"

The bed was still made, and the light in the bathroom wasn't on. He clearly wasn't in here.

Now I had to find him before I'd be able to sleep. "Garrett?" Grateful for my fuzzy socks, I padded through the first floor. When I didn't find him, I stepped out onto the porch.

We hadn't gotten any more snow after the flurries this morning, but we still had a chance. Stadtburg had gotten considerably more, and I probably would've closed the shop before noon because when it snowed, people stayed home.

I walked from one end of the long patio to the other. It was still too early to panic. He wouldn't have left the house without saying anything.

That man better not be driving after taking that pill. I ran out to the garage. My car was right where I'd left it.

The second floor had five bedrooms, and Garrett wasn't in any of them. I pushed open the double doors in the game room and checked the second-floor porch. He wasn't here either.

There was only one place left to check; then I'd panic. The door at the end of the hall stood open. Why hadn't I noticed that? I climbed the circular staircase, then stepped out onto the rooftop patio.

Garrett sat on the sofa with a blanket wrapped around him.

"There you are." I crossed my arms, wishing I'd grabbed a jacket.

"Oh, hey. I thought you'd be asleep by now." He glanced back and smiled. "What do you need?"

"I remembered that you hadn't eaten in hours, and it's better to take your meds with food." I shivered and rubbed my arms.

"I grabbed a doughnut, but thanks for looking out for me."

Lingering near the door, I stared at the back of his head. "What are you doing up here?"

"Thinking."

Answers like that only made me more curious. I sat down beside him. "About?"

He turned to face me. "You."

In the moonlight, I could just make out his smile. Silence surrounded us while I waited for him to elaborate, but he didn't.

Holding out his arm, he motioned me closer. "This blanket is big enough for both of us. Look out that direction."

I stared at the twinkling stars. "The clouds went away."

He wrapped the blanket around my shoulders. "They did."

Fireworks lit up the sky.

I tilted my head to look up at him. "Wow! How did you know?"

"The amusement park does displays sometimes on the weekends. During the summer, I think they do one every night."

I tucked my feet up beside me and leaned against Garrett. "I can't remember the last time I watched a fireworks display."

"That's because you go to bed before the sun goes down most nights." He nudged me and grinned. "This house is nice, but this is the one part I wish I could take home with me. It's almost magical sitting up here and looking out at this view."

"For me, it would be the hot tub." I kept my eyes focused on the sky, enjoying the splashes of color exploding against the darkness.

"You never told me about your family." He shifted and draped his arm around my shoulders.

Right now, I didn't care about the friend zone. I could tell myself I was only snuggled here because the air was frigid, but that would be lying. And I was horrible at making a lie believable. Being alone with Garrett like this felt comfortable. And this week, I was going to let myself enjoy it. I didn't care about any zone.

Life would settle back into normal once he returned home to the ranch and I went back to making doughnuts every morning.

"My parents married really young. Mom was seventeen. Dad was nineteen. They'd dated all through high school and then married a week after her graduation. My earliest memory is of my mom screaming at my dad. Standing toe to toe with him and yelling right in his face. And they've continued that way ever since. Sometimes, it's Dad who does the yelling. They never hit each other, so that's good, I guess."

"I'm sorry you had to grow up with that."

When the fireworks ended, I rested my head on his shoulder. "They both worked, so I stayed with my aunt during the day, Eli's mom. Aunt Patsy always wore a smile, and she had the best laugh. She was a cookies-after-school kind of mom. I love my parents, but being around them isn't enjoyable. Oh, I also forgot to mention the houseful of pets. My parents have seven cats—named after the dwarves—a chihuahua named Diablo, and the dumbest chocolate lab on the planet. Her name is Coco."

He rubbed my shoulder. "Are you a cat or a dog person?"

"I'm a neither. I don't hate them. I just have no desire to have a pet. That probably makes me sound like a horrible person."

"Not at all. Do you get home often?"

"Often enough. I was on my way home from their house when I found you. They moved out near Johnson City several years ago, so I see them a few times a year. They work; I work. But I drove out to have Thanksgiving dinner with them. It was more of a lunch."

"You closed the shop?" There was a hint of tease in his question.

"I closed early. I only stay open until eleven on holidays."

He blinked before looking down at me. "You're open every single day?"

"Yeah. That's too much, isn't it?"

"Yes, Tessa, it's too much."

77

"Delaney told me the same thing." I picked at a piece of lint on the blanket. "I should probably change that."

He rested his head on mine.

"Why were you out on Thanksgiving? Didn't Ava have a big dinner at the ranch?" I wanted to keep him talking because if he went to sleep up here, I'd be in trouble.

"We ate early. I didn't miss it. But I left after we ate because my client had left me a message about her husband." He quieted with his head still against mine.

The wind gusted, and I snuggled closer to him. It would be too easy to fall asleep beside him.

Wriggling my hand out of the blanket, I reached up and touched his face. "Please don't go to sleep. I can't carry you down the stairs. And if we sleep out here, we'll freeze."

His cheek moved against my hand as he smiled. "I'm not falling asleep. I was contemplating an idea."

"What idea?"

"I'm not trying to pull you away from your family, but what if you took a few days off at Christmas and stayed out at the ranch? The cabin by mine is empty. It could be like a mini vacation."

Was it cold enough to freeze tears? I was about to find out. Worrying my bottom lip, I imagined spending Christmas with people who laughed. Then I imagined spending it with Garrett. "I don't know."

"You don't have to decide right now. The offer stands."

"If you feel like retracting it by the end of the week, I'll understand." I managed to get the words out without a waver in my voice, but my favorite spy could probably tell I was about to cry.

Warmth tickled my ear as he leaned in close. "We're friends. Nothing will change that."

How did he know the right words to say? "Thank you."

"Let's get back inside before we turn into icicles." He slipped out from under the blanket and held out his hand. "I've kept you up past your bedtime."

Going into my own room spawned a sense of loneliness, but sleeping snuggled against Garrett simply because I liked how it felt was not allowed in the friend zone even with the most generous of definitions. With my bedroom door open, I slipped under the covers and closed my eyes.

* * *

I OPENED MY EYES, expecting daylight, but the house was still dark. After tapping my phone screen, I groaned. Why was I awake at one in the morning?

Shouts sounded across the hall. Garrett yelled something unintelligible.

My bare feet slapped the cold tile as I raced to his bed.

Flailing and groaning, he fought an unseen assailant.

I scurried across the massive bed on my hands and knees and leaned over him. Was it bad to wake someone during a nightmare?

Instead of shaking him, I laid my head on his chest. "I'm here. You're okay."

He dropped his arms and sighed. "Please don't shoot."

"It's just me, Garrett." Tears stung my eyes, and I wiped them away when they slid down my cheeks. Without lifting my head, I shifted under the covers.

He rested his brace on my back. "Tessa."

"That's right. It's me. I'm just going to stay here to fight off your bad dreams, okay?"

His soft snore sounded a lot like a yes.

Listening to the steady rhythm of his heartbeat, I scolded myself. Less than thirty-six hours into our little getaway, and

I'd tossed my heart onto the butchering slab. I needed to return it to the freezer and tell Garrett that he was right about what I wouldn't do or, more accurately, what I couldn't do. I'd never told anyone before, but he deserved to know why.

CHAPTER 9

J woke up to an empty bed and whistling echoing down the hall. His mouth was healing. That spawned thought tangents I opted not to chase.

Without bothering to change clothes or even pull on socks, I rushed out to the kitchen. "Good morning."

"Hey there. Have a seat. I hope you like breakfast tacos."

"You don't have to cook for me."

He held up his hands. "I didn't. But when I feel a little better, I will. I had breakfast delivered."

"Thank you. Sorry I slept late."

"No reason to apologize." He pulled foiled-wrapped tacos out of a bag. "What happened last night? I'm not saying it wasn't a nice surprise to wake up with you cuddled beside me, but we didn't start out that way."

I perched on a barstool at the counter. "You were having a bad dream and shouting. When I laid my head on your chest, you calmed down. I wanted you to be able to sleep peacefully, so I stayed."

"What did I say?" He winced as he reached into the cabinet for plates.

"I didn't understand most of it, just the part where you asked me not to shoot you." I swiped at my eyes. "You never mentioned that he had a gun."

"I wouldn't have gotten in his truck otherwise." He touched my hand. "After my appointment tomorrow, I'll call the officer from the other night and give him more info."

"That's probably a good idea." I carried the platter of tacos to the table, then whipped around to look at Garrett. "You took off your bandage."

"Yeah. The scrapes are healing." He pulled mugs out of the cabinet. "Coffee?"

"Please. Lots of cream and lots of sugar."

He laughed. "I'll let you fix it. I'm not sure how much qualifies as lots."

After perfecting my coffee, I picked up two tacos.

"I wasn't sure what kind you liked, so there are a few different ones. And I won't be bothered if you switch those out for something else." He watched as I unwrapped my tacos.

"I'm not sure there is a bad kind of breakfast taco."

"Very true." He picked up three and tore away the foil. "There is supposed to be a meteor shower tonight, so if you can stay awake, we could go up to the roof again."

"I'd like that." It was irrational to have feelings for a man who I'd only known for seventy-two hours. Well, I'd known him longer than that because I'd met him weeks ago, but still. We hadn't spent much time together before I'd picked him up off the side of the road. Attraction and infatuation. That was all this was.

He'd probably agree with me. The only reason he'd wanted to kiss me was because I'd helped him and because it was a perfectly romantic scene with us snuggled in the hot tub. Those were the reasons.

I ate way too many tacos before finally pushing away from the table. "That was so good. Thank you."

"You're welcome. You've been amazing. This was the least I could do."

I refilled my coffee and mixed in more cream and sugar. "I found a battleship game and a deck of cards upstairs. Want to play a game?"

"Sure."

Garrett picked up the plates, and it was obvious from how he moved that he was still in pain. "I've got the kitchen. Go enjoy your free time."

I thought about his words. "I don't know what to do. I rarely have free time. I man the shop, run errands, make dinner, and sleep. And I get together with Delaney and Eli sometimes." I reached for a rag. "I can just—"

He set the plates down and stood in front of me. "No, Tessa. I'll clean up."

"But you're in pain. I can tell."

"I'll live. I'm putting away leftovers and throwing away trash. Go pretend like this is a vacation."

"You've given me something to think about." I brushed at a spot of salsa on his shirt.

"Me?"

Honesty was the best policy, but it often landed me in uncomfortable situations. "I've been thinking about you since you landed on top of me in the ditch."

Before he could tease me, I hurried back to the bedroom. I had a book to read. Why wouldn't I want to read about a happy couple kissing and falling in love? This was turning out to be a frustrating week. And it wasn't even Monday.

* * *

83

WHEN IT WAS time to go up to the roof, I filled mugs with hot chocolate and followed Garrett to the patio sofa. He only grabbed one blanket, which meant we'd have to share again. I didn't mind that.

Cuddled beside him and staring at the sky, I sipped my hot chocolate. I probably wouldn't get a better time than right now to explain why I wasn't open to the idea of a relationship. "Garrett, last night when you said that about what I wouldn't do, you were right."

He nodded. "I know. It wasn't just an educated guess. Weeks ago, when I asked you out, you told me you didn't date." After a sip of his hot chocolate, he looked at me. "And I'm guessing that the reason for that is related to the reason you were so upset about waking up next to me Saturday morning."

"Being a mind reader must've really helped with the investigator gig." I pulled my knees up to my chest. "I started dating a guy my senior year of high school. He was two years ahead of me."

"I bet your parents hated that."

"Oh, yeah. Even though it was exactly like them, or maybe *because* it was exactly like them. But Skeeter—that was his nickname—and I dated for a year before he asked me to marry him. I'd only been out of high school a short time, so we scheduled the wedding for the following year. I worked at the doughnut shop. Mrs. Sweet owned it then. I'm not making that up. And I loved it. She taught me how to make doughnuts. We made up new flavors together. That was a wonderful year. Then about two months before the wedding, she didn't show up one morning. I made the doughnuts and covered the morning rush, then closed the shop to go check on her." I used the blanket to wipe my face. "She had a heart attack. A neighbor found her, but she didn't make it." Warm cocoa soothed me as I regained my composure.

Garrett wrapped his arm around me. "She sounds like a cookies-after-school kind of person."

"She was wonderful. And she left me the shop. That's how I ended up with my own business at twenty. And I promised her I'd make it a success."

A shooting star streaked across the dark sky, and I wished that my heart had never been broken beyond repair.

"I think you've kept that promise."

"I left out a part. After Skeeter and I were engaged, he got more persistent about wanting to... sleep together. And I don't mean in the same bed. He wanted me to—"

"I get it, Tessa."

"Sorry. Of course you do. Anyway, I didn't want to, and eventually he backed off. Just stopped bringing it up."

Garrett groaned.

"Yeah. Well, about three weeks before the wedding, he was over one night and brought it up again. He kept pushing and talking about how we were so close to the wedding date." I pulled in a deep breath. "So, I slept with him. He was my fiancé, and I felt like I owed him that."

Garrett pulled me closer. "That's not the way that works."

I struggled to maintain my composure. "No one knows I did that, so please don't tell anyone."

"I won't."

"When I woke up the next morning, Skeeter was already gone. He'd slipped out during the night." This blanket was going to be soaked by the time I finished my story. "He came into the shop as the morning rush subsided and pulled me aside. There weren't many people in the shop, thankfully. And we were tucked in a corner. Anyway, Skeeter started the conversation by asking for the ring back. I made the mistake of asking why. He admitted that he'd been seeing other women, and he said that..." I couldn't make the words leave my mouth.

Garrett closed his eyes, his thumb rubbing circles on my shoulder.

We sat in silence for a few seconds.

"He compared me to the other women, and said I wasn't very good. I was inexperienced and couldn't compete with the ladies who'd practiced a lot. I'm paraphrasing. I'll spare you the way he said it."

Garrett tensed. "I hope I never meet him."

"After he left, I closed the shop, took all the doughnuts with me to my apartment, and ate myself sick. I didn't open the shop again for a week. But I'd sneak back and make doughnuts during the night so that I'd have enough for the following day."

"That's why you knew Eli and Delaney would be concerned."

"I knew Eli would be. Delaney doesn't know the whole story. She might now. Eli doesn't know about the night before. He only knows Skeeter broke up with me." I blinked, hoping the tears would stop burning my eyes.

"Probably best to keep Eli in the dark about that part."

"When I finally did open, people kept coming in to tell me about how they were sorry and how they knew Skeeter had been seeing this person and that person. Because of the town gossip, I learned how much I'd been cheated on. I ate as many doughnuts as I sold for the next two months. Which was horrible for business and for my health. I put on a lot of weight then. I was almost unrecognizable."

"That's why you don't eat doughnuts."

Avoiding eye contact, I nodded. "I woke up one morning and decided to move on. I stopped eating doughnuts and gave up the idea of dating. That was seven years ago. Most people that know I don't date think it's because I'm afraid of falling in love. That's not it. I'm afraid of what comes after. And by avoiding romantic relationships, I never have to make myself vulnerable in that way again. I can't risk ever feeling that way again. So, I just stick to what I'm good at. Does that even make sense?" I braved a look at him.

He stared out at the sky. "It makes sense."

His words added to my ache. If one man thought I wasn't good, most men would probably agree. My admission might even change the nature of our friendship, but he deserved to know, no matter the outcome.

"Maybe I should just let you—"

Garrett pulled me close. "I knew when I asked you to stay here that you didn't date. It's part of the reason I didn't kiss you. And if you'd told me this story weeks ago, I still would've asked you to sit with me on this roof and watch the stars." The wind blew, and he pulled the blanket around us tighter. "Where does it say that only people who are dating can spend time together? I'm not asking you to kiss me. I'm not asking you to—"

"Don't say it."

He chuckled, but it didn't have its usual ring. "You are the most giving person I know. And I don't say that lightly. Given what I know now, I think you edged out Ava when you helped me get my jeans off."

I covered my face with my hands, forgetting I had a half-full mug of lukewarm chocolate in one of them. Chocolate splashed all over me and the blanket just as the mug whapped me in the face. Laughing, I wiped my face with the blanket, which wasn't much help. "Oh, ouch. Now we'll have matching bruises."

"Need me to lick that chocolate off you?"

"Garrett! Friends don't do that."

He wrapped his arms around my waist. "*We* decide what we do as friends. Outside rules do not apply."

"I never thought of it that way."

He kissed my forehead. "You let me know what's okay.

And I won't push beyond that. Ever. But if at some point in the future, you change your mind about what you want our friendship to look like, please tell me."

I hugged him, then pulled back when he tensed. "Sorry. I forgot about your ribs."

"Let's get you inside before you turn into a fudgsicle." He helped me up, then gathered the blanket into his arms.

With a mug in each hand, I started toward the stairs. "I'm going to take a quick shower and wash the chocolate off. Alone." I added the last part, hoping to get a laugh.

"So, you're saying that showering together isn't okay for us as friends?" He winked. "Glad that's been cleared up."

Now I was excited about the rest of the week and even about the days beyond that. He'd listened to me unload my secret, and our friendship remained unchanged.

This week wasn't so bad.

CHAPTER 10

*G*arrett glanced up from his magazine when I tapped his arm. "Yes?"

"Don't forget to ask the doctor if it's okay for you to take your brace off to shower."

"Hopefully it is considering I've already done that, but I'll ask." He turned the page.

"And about how many times a day you should ice your hand to help the swelling. I'm not sure we've been doing that enough." I'd written out a list of questions, then left the house without them, so I was trying to remind Garrett of all the questions that needed to be asked.

"I have a better idea. You ask the doctor. Come back there with me."

I glanced at the receptionist, hoping she wasn't eaves-dropping on our conversation. "I'm not sure if they'll even let me, Garrett. I'm not your… anything."

"I'm pretty sure they aren't going to ask about our rela-tionship status, Tessa."

A nurse stepped into a doorway. "Garrett Wright."

Garrett closed his magazine and laid it on the table. "That's us."

I walked toward the door, trying to figure out what explanation I'd give if the nurse asked why I was back there. Saying that I was Garrett's caregiver for the week wasn't a lie. Or I could go with a simpler explanation and tell her I was Garrett's friend. Perhaps, I was overthinking this a bit.

We made it all the way back to the room without her asking us anything.

"The doctor will be with you in a moment." She closed the door on her way out.

I didn't even have time to remind Garrett about another question before the doctor walked in.

"Hello, I'm Dr. Palmer." His eyebrows shot up when he saw Garrett's face. "Looks like you ran into a bit of trouble."

"I did."

The doctor opened the folder in his hand and flipped through the pages inside. "Is this your wife?" He didn't look up as he asked the question.

"No. Tessa's here as a favor. I know I won't remember everything."

"All right then. Let's have a look." The doctor focused on Garrett's scraped-up hand. "Tell me what happened."

"Someone slammed it against a brick wall. Then dragged it across the brick." Garrett seemed so calm.

As he explained more of what happened to the doctor, I learned details that hadn't previously been mentioned.

Dr. Palmer poked around, moving Garrett's hand while trying to avoid touching the wounds. "We'll need to x-ray that one. What about the other hand?" He pulled off Garrett's brace and repeated the poking and prodding.

Garrett shot me a side glance. "Used it to stop my fall when I was tossed out of a truck."

"Ouch." The doctor scribbled in the chart, then stood. "X-rays will let us see what's broken. The nurse will take you over there." He closed the folder. "Any questions for me?"

"Can she go with me for the X-rays?" Garrett laid his hand on mine.

"Absolutely. We have a fabulous machine that lets us see inside your hand as you move. It shows up on a monitor. I'll have the nurse pull up a chair for her, and she can be next to you." The doctor nodded before walking out of the room.

"Was it moving when they tossed you out?" I stared at his battered hand.

"Yep, but not at full speed. I wasn't thinking about what I'd have to tell the doctor when I asked you to come back here with me. I'm sorry."

I leaned my head on his shoulder. "Don't apologize. I can handle it."

Forty-five minutes later, Garrett had a brace on his left hand, but his right hand, thankfully, had no broken bones. And his road rash was healed enough that the bandages were no longer necessary.

For a Monday, the day wasn't turning out to be bad.

GARRETT LIFTED A COUCH CUSHION. "Have you seen my phone?"

"It's on your nightstand, but it probably needs to be charged." I finished chopping vegetables before glancing up. "Why?"

"I want to call the deputy." He walked down the hall, then returned, carrying his phone and a charger. "I put his number in my phone the day you picked up my truck. I don't think I've touched this thing since."

I pushed my phone across the counter. "Use mine. His card is in my purse."

"No. I'll use my phone." He plugged it in. "It's charging."

Garrett had a stubborn side, and this afternoon, it was on full display.

After washing my hands, I pulled the card out of my purse. "Why does it matter what phone you use?"

He leaned on the counter, his jaw tight. "Because even though I was on pain medication, I saw the way that guy looked at you, and I don't want *your number* in *his phone*. That's why it matters."

"Seriously? He was probably looking at me like that because I was sitting next to the bed of someone I told him I didn't know. Because I talked to him before I knew that I knew you." I tossed the veggies onto a baking sheet. "I doubt I could've made that sound any more confusing."

"Made perfect sense to me, but I'm not taking any chances." He opened his laptop. "Want to play another game of cards later?"

"Sure. But I'm not going to let you beat me this time."

He walked up behind me and brushed his stubble on my neck. "Let me beat you? Really? That's funny, Tessa."

"Are you saying I'm lying?"

"I don't have to. It's written all over your face."

Heat rushed to my cheeks and every other part of me. "Even if you always win, I still want to play cards with you."

He cupped my cheek. "I know I've said it a lot, and by the end of the week, I will have said it a lot more, but thank you for everything—amazing food, incredible care, and friendship. Even sore, I'm enjoying this getaway."

I wrapped my arms around his neck and hugged him gently. "I'm sorry you got hurt, but this has been fun. Getting to know you has been the best part. You're hurting today, aren't you?"

Nodding, he rubbed my back, then tightened his embrace. "I'm really glad we're friends."

I was beginning to think the zone for our friendship was approximately the same size as Texas. Big. Maybe even as big as Alaska.

* * *

WAKING up at one in the morning was happening all too frequently. I lay in bed, wondering why there was a light on in the living room. Garrett typically turned them all off before he went to bed.

Was he still up? Had he woken up because of a nightmare?

I pulled on my fuzzy socks before walking down the hall. "You're still up."

"Yeah." He snapped his laptop closed and set it on the coffee table. "I was trying to be quiet. Sorry."

I shook my head as I sat down beside him. "You didn't wake me. I just woke up. Are you working my case?"

"No, a side project." He laid a throw pillow in his lap. "Stretch out. I'll turn on a movie."

"How are you even awake?" I lay down on my side and pulled a throw over me.

He patted my hip. "Just am."

While he searched for something to watch, I closed my eyes. The next thing I knew, Garrett nudged my shoulder.

"I'd carry you to bed, but my abs aren't up to it yet." His lips brushed my temple. "I'm going to turn in."

I wasn't sure being kissed like that fit in most people's friend zone, but it felt nice. I reminded myself not to say that out loud. "Did you enjoy the movie?"

"I fell asleep. When I almost tipped over on top of you, I decided it was time to go to bed." He rubbed my back as I sat up.

I shuffled down the hall. "Wake me if you need anything."

He stayed in my doorway until I was tucked in bed. "Same. Good night."

When it came to sleep schedules, we were as different as night and day.

CHAPTER 11

$\mathscr{H}$olding my bathrobe closed, I opened the front door. "Officer Gomez, you're early. Come on in. Garrett should be out in a minute or two."

The guy filled up the doorway, and his gaze fixed on me. It dropped ever so slightly, but only for half a second. "You?" He closed his eyes and rubbed two fingers up and down on his forehead. "I'm confused. At the hospital, you said you didn't know this guy and that he was a stranger who you'd picked up off the side of the road. And—"

"Oh, I haven't talked to you since—"

He put up a hand. "Let me finish."

I sighed and forced a smile. "Go ahead."

"You did say that y'all had a *bond*." He added air quotes, which just irritated me. "I wasn't too surprised to find you in his hospital room, but here? That's some bond."

"Are you coming in or not? As my dad would say, we don't want to heat the entire town."

He stepped inside.

I slammed the door. "Are you finished now?"

Nodding, he scanned the house. "Nice place."

"Because of how beat up he was, I didn't recognize Garrett. And for reasons I *will not* explain to you, I'm staying here and helping him as he recovers."

His lips curled into a smile. "The reasons seem pretty obvious."

Fire raged inside, and I let go of the robe and popped my hands onto my hips. "You don't know *squat*."

He stared at my swimsuit a second before his gaze snapped to something over my shoulder.

"I see you've met Tessa." Garrett walked up and pointed at the kitchen counter. "Why don't we have a seat over there?"

Officer Gomez nodded in my direction. "Miss Best." Then he strolled to the counter.

Garrett lifted his eyebrows. "You okay?"

I shrugged, then blew out a breath, half expecting to see flames. "He's pompous and aggravating. Did you hear the implication dripping from his words?" I kept my voice at a whisper because I wasn't going to give Deputy Dense the satisfaction of hearing me gripe. "I'm going to run back and change."

"I'll talk to him." Garrett bumped my hand.

"Thank you."

In record time, I changed and ran back toward the living room but stopped before the guys spotted me.

"This house isn't mine. It's a rental. We're only staying here a week. For personal reasons as I explained the other day, I don't want my family to know about my injuries right now, and Tessa is helping me. Until yesterday, I could barely use my hands." Garrett made it all sound so reasonable and nothing like the officer had implied.

"Are you serious? She finds you on the side of a road and agrees to spend a week with you? Just like that? Dang."

Officer Gomez chuckled. "I want to know where I can sign up for that."

I peeked out to see Garrett's reaction, but I wasn't sure why that mattered to me.

His face looked like it was carved out of stone. "Listen. I think you've gotten the wrong idea."

The steel in his voice sent a shiver down my spine.

"Tessa and I are *friends*." Garrett leaned forward. "Am I clear?"

The deputy nodded. "Sorry. I didn't mean to imply… anything."

"Back to the reason I called." Garrett crossed his arms.

I strolled out and transferred the last few doughnuts to a platter. "Coffee?"

"That'd be great. Thanks, Tessa." Garrett picked up a doughnut then nudged the platter across the counter. "Officer Gomez?"

"Call me Nico. And I'd like coffee also. Thank you."

Garrett pointed at the platter. "She makes doughnuts for a living. These are the best. No pun intended."

Nico grinned as he chose a doughnut. "Before we get to why you called. A funny thing happened. Just before I left the office, a woman called in asking me to do a well-check on you. Says she saw her husband beating you up. She worried you might be dead on the side of the road somewhere."

I almost dropped a mug. "Is she trying to get her husband arrested?"

It was easier to focus on that than on the idea of Garrett being dead on the side of the road. Blinking away tears, I grabbed milk out of the fridge.

"Maybe that's her game." Garrett shook his head. "She's called my phone about fifty times since Friday, but she hasn't left a message."

"What she did doesn't excuse the beating you got. Are you

sure you don't want to press charges?" Nico glanced at me, then focused on Garrett.

"He accused me of stalking his wife and laying hands on her, so I'm not sure what she told him. She lit his fuse. I won't press charges."

"Fair enough." Nico set his doughnut down. "You are right about these being the best. Where is your shop, Tessa?"

Garrett tucked an arm around my waist as I slid mugs onto the counter. "It's in Stadtburg."

I stirred sugar into my coffee. "What he said."

"I'll have to remember that." Nico sipped his coffee. "Tell me more about what the woman said when she hired you."

I stayed beside Garrett as he explained. Later, I'd tease him about the timing of putting his arm around me. I was pretty sure that was his guy signal, telling Nico to leave me alone. I didn't mind. If I were going to break my no-dating rule, Garrett was who I'd go out with.

Poor Nico was going to leave here more confused than when he arrived, but after the way he acted at the door, I didn't feel bad about that.

* * *

TWO DAYS LATER, Garrett stared at his phone as it rang. "I'm not going to answer that, but maybe this time she'll leave a message."

When the ringing stopped, I held my breath and waited to see if a voice mail notification popped up.

The phone buzzed, and he snatched it off the table, then played the message on speaker.

The voice of the she-devil echoed in the room. "Mr. Wright, I'm very concerned about you. Please call the county sheriff's office and ask for Nico Gomez. He's handling the case, and you can talk to him about pressing charges. Please contact him soon." The message ended without an apology for what had happened.

"She is heartless." I patted Garrett's shoulder. "I'm so sorry."

He forwarded the voice mail to Nico. "He can take care of it. Hot tub or rooftop?"

If I couldn't see that the phone call had stressed him, the question would've given it away.

"The roof. I'll grab a blanket."

"I'll make popcorn." He strode into the kitchen.

I hated seeing him upset, but it was clear why he was bothered. If I wanted to pluck out the woman's eyelashes and shove staples under her fingernails—not that I would actually do those things—I could only imagine how Garrett felt.

Ten minutes later, he sat down next to me on the patio sofa. "What are we going to talk about?"

I tapped him to lean forward, then wrapped the blanket around both of us. "I want you to check with everyone at the ranch before I give a final yes, but if they are fine with it, I'll take off a few days and spend Christmas out there. Technically, I could stay open and just drive out there after work, but I'm starting to like having days off."

"Good. It'll be fun. What about your parents?"

"I'll run up and see them one evening. My mom has been hounding me about getting out and doing more, so she'll be thrilled if I tell her that I'm going to spend Christmas with a friend. She'll be extra excited to learn that friend is a guy."

He laughed. "I think you'll enjoy it. Ava makes so many desserts. You can help her, I bet. I mean… if you want to."

I pulled a handful of popcorn out of the bowl. "Cooking and baking with Ava would be fun."

"Eating what you make would be even more fun." He ate some popcorn. "What are we going to do for fun without a rooftop patio and a hot tub? Well, we'll still have access to a hot tub. Dad has one."

"We might have to make use of that. We could watch movies. Take walks."

"There are lots of beautiful spaces on the ranch. We can definitely walk. As far as movies... so far, I think you've stayed awake through only one. The one where they kissed at the end."

I leaned into his shoulder. "That's why I stayed awake. For the good stuff."

He grinned as he grabbed another handful of popcorn. Then he grew serious. "I don't think I want to continue being a private investigator."

"I don't blame you. It's dangerous." I didn't want him to continue being a private investigator, but what right did I have to tell him that?

"I need to heal a bit more, but I think I'm going to tell Dad that I want to learn about ranching." Garrett stared at the blanket.

I moved the popcorn bowl to the table, then shifted to face him. "I think that's wonderful. You'll make a great cowboy."

"Right. I know nothing about cows or horses or where to buy hay." He shot me a side glance. "This will be challenging."

I brushed his cheek, careful not to press on his bruises. "You're protective, honest, and kind. You have more integrity in your pinky finger than some men have in their entire body. That's what will make you a good cowboy. A truck, jeans, and a hat help, but you already have jeans and a truck. And you'll rock the hat."

"How do you know so much about cowboys? Was Skeeter a cowboy?"

We hadn't talked about Skeeter since that night up here on the roof.

"He had a truck and a hat, but no integrity." I shivered when the wind blew.

Garrett put an arm around me. "Where is he now?"

"Around. He married and settled down in a small town near Stadtburg. His wife and kids come into the doughnut shop from time to time."

"It must be hard seeing him." Garrett's tone was tender.

"It was for a while mostly because I was embarrassed and felt rejected. But realizing he wasn't a prize helped squash those feelings. I don't care about Skeeter. I haven't for a long time."

"You deserve a prize."

When he said things like that, hope sparked, but then like a bucket of cold water, Skeeter's words, which played on repeat in my head, washed all the hope away.

I needed a new topic. "Your dad is going to be excited about you taking up ranching."

Garrett pulled me closer. Was it wrong to like a person because they were always warm?

"I think you're right. But when I have a hard day and feel like I made the wrong choice, I'm coming to you."

I patted his chest. "And I'll give you a doughnut and a pep talk. Any time. That's what friends are for."

* * *

I'D FALLEN asleep while watching a movie again and woke up in Garrett's bed, but I was alone. This week had been amazing, but it was almost over. I wasn't ready for it to end. Spending time with Garrett and redefining what friendship looked like had ripped the bandage off some of my wounds. I was quick to tell people I was happy, but having a happy-face bandage covering up the pain wasn't the same as happy.

That was the hard lesson I'd learned this week. What I hadn't figured out was if the wounds could ever heal.

Stretching, I wandered out to the kitchen.

"Hey there. Have a seat. The pancakes are almost ready. And the bacon"—he peeked into the oven—"needs about two more minutes."

"You don't have to cook for me."

He flipped a pancake, then focused those baby blues on me. "You made it through the first half of the movie last night."

I perched on a barstool at the counter. "You didn't wake me up so that I could crawl into my bed."

"I'm going to miss snuggling with you and watching movies." He went back to making pancakes.

"I'll miss it too." I blinked so he wouldn't notice the mist in my eyes. "How are you feeling? You seem better."

"My ribs are still sore, but not nearly as bad today. My face feels much better but looks horrible." He turned off the stove and pulled the bacon out of the oven. "I think that cream is helping the pain and bruising."

"I can put it on again after your shower." I carried the platter to the table, then whipped around to look at Garrett. "If you want."

"That would be great. Thanks." He pulled mugs out of the cabinet. "Coffee?"

"Please."

He fixed my coffee with lots of cream and sugar, just how I liked it.

"Thank you." I drizzled maple syrup over my short stack. "These look good. I'm impressed."

"You haven't tasted them yet. You might not be as impressed after you do." He broke a slice of bacon in half. "Want to soak in the hot tub for a bit after breakfast?"

"Yes, I do." I popped a bite of pancakes into my mouth and

moaned. "Oh my gosh. Where did you learn to make pancakes like this? They are like yummy clouds."

"My grandma." Garrett beamed. "I'm glad you like them."

This perfect little bubble was about to pop, so I tried to soak up joy out of every last second.

CHAPTER 12

I blinked, trying to clear the tears out of my eyes before Garrett caught me crying. It was silly to be getting emotional about the end of our stay. The week was over.

Folding my clothes, I thought through what needed to be done before opening the shop tomorrow. The refrigerator would need to be cleaned out, and the whole place would need to be scrubbed. I had my work cut out for me.

Garrett slipped up behind me and rested his chin on my shoulder. "Do we have time for a *friendly* hot tub soak?" Was he trying to delay our departure?

I wasn't opposed to a delay. "We have to be out of here in less than two hours. So, we'd only have time for a short soak."

"Good thing I already have my suit on." He flopped onto the bed. "I'm feeling so much better. My bruises are nasty colors, but moving and breathing aren't chores anymore." He wiggled the fingers sticking out of the end of his brace. "And this brace lets me use my fingers. I hated that other one. I really missed using my fingers. It wasn't that I didn't like being fed, but it's different."

Laughing, I shoved the last few things into my bag. "I'm really glad you're feeling better." I sat down beside him and stared at his lips, imagining how they'd feel pressed to mine. What was I doing? Yanking myself back to reality, I jumped up and pulled my swimsuit—that I'd just packed—out of my bag. "Give me a second to change."

"I'll meet you out there."

We'd gotten a great deal of use out of that hot tub this week, especially considering that it was cold. There was a lot I'd miss about our little getaway, but the long conversations in the hot tub and on the roof were absolutely at the top of the list.

I'd enjoyed myself more than I thought possible, and it was because Garrett had let me decide what our friendship would look like. Not once during the week had he asked me to reconsider my promise. Around him, I could be myself. I didn't have to risk anything.

A small part of me feared that leaving here would change our friendship.

I slipped on the robe and padded out to the hot tub, ready to eke as much friendship out of the week as I could get.

Easing into the water, I took one last opportunity to enjoy gazing at his chest. Even if it did have funny-colored bruises on it. "What kinds of cookies do you like? What kinds did your grandma make?" Selfishly, I stopped in front of him, knowing he'd wrap his arms around me.

He did. "My grandma made a mean snickerdoodle cookie. But I think my favorite is the good old-fashioned chocolate chip cookie."

"Soft or crunchy?"

He rubbed his whiskers on my neck. "Soft. That's not even a question."

For the next forty-five minutes, we covered a range of

topics. Both of us were stalling. Neither of us wanted to leave.

I leaned back and kissed his cheek. "Thanks for a great week. If we don't leave soon, they'll charge you for another day, and it will mess up someone else's schedule." I walked to the stairs. "What time does your dad arrive?"

"They flew in last night. I had my dates wrong." Garrett followed me into the house. "You can join us for dinner if you'd like. Ava always makes more than enough."

"Not tonight because I have to get the shop ready, but I might take you up on that one night. Don't say anything to them, but now that Delaney and Eli are engaged, I spend more evenings by myself. I know they don't care if I hang out with them, but I don't want to be in the way."

"You are welcome on the ranch any time."

* * *

GARRETT TOSSED his bag into the truck, then turned to face me. Goodbye seemed like it would be easy when I said yes to this week, but now my chest tightened. I would not cry about this.

He brushed my cheek.

Okay, so maybe I'd cry a little.

"I'd like to cash in that raincheck for a hug now." He opened his arms.

Instead of reminding him that I'd hugged him more than once during the week, I reminded myself not to squeeze him too hard. It was silly to be upset. He lived ten minutes away. With my face buried in the curve of his neck, I held him. "I'm glad I didn't run over you on the side of the road."

"You and me both." With one hand on my back, he threaded his fingers into my hair with the other. "I've pelted you with thank-yous all week, but I'll say it again. Thank you for playing nurse, for closing your shop to take care of me, but mostly for being my friend. Texas feels a little more like home now."

"You're welcome." I pulled back and wiped my eyes. "Usually I rotate my specialty flavors, but the pecan praline doughnuts will now be available every day."

"I'll remember that." He cupped my cheek and smiled before letting me go and climbing into his truck. "See you later."

It was good I had work to do at the shop. I desperately needed a distraction.

I tossed my bag inside the apartment, then drove to the shop. After my normal closing time, I'd take down my handwritten sign, but for now, I'd stay closed and clean up. Four was going to feel really early tomorrow morning. I hadn't exactly stayed on my normal schedule this week.

The rest of the afternoon, I replenished ingredients and cleaned. I guessed that once word spread that I was open again, doughnut-craving locals would swarm to the shop. That would help make up for the lost revenue.

Not surprisingly, five minutes after Delaney's store closed, she knocked on the front door.

"Hey there. I was hoping you'd stop by." I was glad I could finally tell her why I'd been gone for a week.

She crossed her arms. "I want to hear about your week. This has to be a good story."

"I am now at liberty to tell you what happened." I went back to sweeping as I talked. "When I was driving home from my parents' house on Thanksgiving, I spilled coffee on myself and pulled over to clean it up. I found Garrett beat up on the side of the road. At the time, I didn't know it was Garrett because his face was really messed up and it was dark. You might want to leave out the part about how I didn't know it was Garrett because if Eli thinks I picked up a stranger—which I totally did—he will give me grief about it."

Delaney didn't say anything, and when I turned to look at her, I laughed.

Her jaw hung open. "You aren't lying. This is really what happened. That's crazy!"

"It was wild. But then when I was trying to help him fill out paperwork at the hospital because he didn't have any ID on him, I figured out who he was. He didn't want anyone at the ranch to know what kind of shape he was in because he didn't want his dad to cut his honeymoon short. They've waited like a year or more to go someplace." I set the broom aside and grabbed the dustpan. "Anyway, I took Garrett back to my apartment, but someone was bound to see him. And Eli wasn't going to leave me alone. He showed up just because I'd closed the shop."

"He was concerned." Delaney made a face. "Really worried because you hadn't closed the shop since... you know."

"Yeah. Well, Garrett rented a house for the week. I made sure he got his meds on time and made us food. We had a nice time."

"And?" She grinned.

"That's it. I don't know what else you want me to say." I didn't give Delaney all the details about the rooftop porch and the private hot tub because I knew that my definition of friendship and hers weren't even in the same dictionary.

Delaney's eyes rolled so far up into her head it looked like it hurt. "We're talking about the tall, muscular Garrett who has those blue eyes, right? Any sparks? Did you kiss him?"

I'd thought about kissing him a lot, but I wasn't going to say that to Delaney. "No, I didn't kiss him. We're friends." I sighed. "You know I don't date. That hasn't changed."

"You haven't dated for seven years. Whatever you were

trying to prove to yourself, I think you've accomplished that. I think you need to leave the past behind and see what's right in front of you." She opened her arms to give me a hug. "The two of y'all would be adorable together. But I'll be quiet about it."

I couldn't tell Delaney that I saw what was in front of me, wanted it more than words could express, but was terrified that I'd be a disappointment. Being heartbroken by a cheater was one thing, but being told I wasn't good enough was rejection on a whole other level. I couldn't handle that twice.

"Thanks. Besides Eli, I haven't really had a guy friend. I thought it would be weird spending a week with Garrett, but it wasn't. Not at all."

"Sometimes you start talking to someone, and it feels like you've been friends for a long time even though it's only been a short time." She smiled. "I get it."

"It is like that. Or at least it was like that this week. Now that we're back to regular life, I probably won't see much of him. He has a life."

"This is a small town. I bet you'll see him." Delaney looked down at her phone. "Eli is on his way to the house. We're going to watch a movie. Want to come?"

"No thanks. I'm going to finish up here and tuck in early. Have fun." The last thing I wanted to do tonight was watch my very happy friends cuddle.

She left, and once again, I was alone with my thoughts. Tonight, there would be no evening hot-tub soak or late-night stargazing. It would just be me alone in my apartment. I'd never minded that before.

* * *

THAT NIGHT as I crawled in bed early enough that Garrett would laugh if he had any idea, my phone buzzed. After settling in and getting my covers smoothed out, I picked up the phone.

Garrett texted: *I wanted to catch you before you went lights out. I've kind of gotten used to telling you good night, so good night, Tessa.*

I tapped out a reply and hit send. *What a nice surprise! Good night to you too. I just tucked in bed so I can be awake early to make the doughnuts.*

See you soon.

His reply had me smiling.

CHAPTER 13

*Y*awning, I ran down my list, glad that I'd taken the time to make it. Getting back into the swing of mornings wasn't easy. Partially because my thoughts kept jumping to Garrett.

The coffee was made. I'd replenished the sugar and the creamer. The case was full of warm doughnuts. And it was time for me to unlock the door.

I flipped the bolt, then turned the sign. Hopefully, word had spread that I was open again. The door opened before I made it to the counter, and I spun around. "Good mor—"

Garrett waved. "Hey."

"Good morning. I'm surprised to see you here this early." I hugged him before hurrying back behind the counter.

"I was hoping if I got here when you opened, the praline doughnuts might still be warm."

I put one on a plate, then picked up a mug. "They are. This is on the house."

"Thanks." He dropped a twenty into my tip jar before filling his coffee mug.

"How did yesterday go for you? I'm guessing the bruises were a bit of a surprise for everyone."

"Oh yeah." He stood at the counter opposite me. "We have to make sure Lilith never finds out that woman's name. I think she might take her down. Ava fussed over me and made one of my favorites for dinner. The guys cursed a lot."

"I bet they did, and I can't blame them. What did Ava make?"

"Enchilada casserole." He bit into his doughnut and moaned. "These are amazing. Every time."

"Have you said anything to your dad yet?"

He shook his head. "No. I'm going to wait a week or two. How was your day?"

"Quiet. Busy. Delaney stopped by and grilled me about my week." I made a funny face, hoping to at least get a chuckle for my efforts.

It worked. "I fielded a few questions myself. Not from Delaney. Ava must've asked if I'd had a nice week at least ten times."

"Good morning." Eli held open the door as Delaney walked in. "I'm glad you took a vacation, but I missed having doughnuts."

Delaney patted his stomach. "It was probably good for you."

Eli stopped and grinned at Garrett. "Hey there. You look like someone took a bat to you."

"Just fists. Mostly. I'm much improved from last Saturday. I'm almost not ugly anymore."

I leaned over the counter and swatted his arm, not hard because that would be rude and because of his bruises. "You were never not handsome."

Garrett lifted his eyebrows. "I thought you didn't lie."

"I'm not lying." I handed Eli and Delaney each a to-go cup and nodded at the coffee station. "Freshly brewed."

When I made eye contact with Delaney, she pressed a hand over her heart and fluttered her eyelashes.

I rolled my eyes and picked up a rag to wipe down counters. Again. Garrett and I were just friends, but that didn't mean I was blind to his good looks. Or his other fantastic qualities. So many of them.

He devoured his doughnut, then sipped his coffee until after Eli and Delaney left. "I should go, but I'll give you a call later maybe."

"Sounds good." Maybe my worries that I wouldn't see him often were unfounded. I hoped so.

THAT EVENING just before I tucked in bed, Mom called.

"Hi, Mom."

"Tessa, I hadn't heard from you and was starting to get a bit worried. You usually don't go an entire week without calling."

"Sorry about that. I ended up spending a week with a friend—"

"A guy?"

"Yes, but he's only a friend. Things were busy." Sort of. Now I felt a little bad for not calling.

"I'm happy to hear you have a new *friend*." The smile in her voice left no doubt I'd be hearing about this again. "I was afraid the squabble your dad and I had at Thanksgiving bothered you."

I pulled the phone away from my ear and stared at it half a second. Mom had never apologized for their arguments before.

"Uh, I… it wasn't that big a deal. I guess I'm used to it." I wanted to retract the words as soon as they left my mouth. That was the wrong thing to say.

Mom sighed. "Sorry about that. I'm trying not to find fault as often. And your dad is trying not to have faults."

"Everyone has faults, Mom."

"It was a joke, sweetheart. Except the trying part. I really am trying."

I had two big reasons for never risking a relationship again. And while Skeeter's words were the biggest chunk of that, Mom and Dad's arguments played a part in my decision. It seemed like one of my reasons was fading a bit.

But that didn't mean my choices had to change.

* * *

ONE WEEK LATER, I pulled onto the ranch, wondering if I should've worn jeans instead of a skirt. I didn't want anyone here thinking this was a date, but the way Garrett talked about everyone on the ranch, I was eager to come for dinner. Was it a crime to want to look nice?

If I planned to spend Christmas here—I still couldn't believe I'd agreed to that, but I wasn't about to change my mind—then it would be good to get to know everyone a little better. That was why I was having dinner at the ranch.

Garrett waved as I parked.

I climbed out of the car and surveyed the main house. "This place is beautiful."

"Come on in. I'll give you a quick tour and show you the hot tub before we join the others in the dining hall." His gaze swept over me. "You look really nice."

"Thanks." I stepped inside as he opened the door.

Hallways branched off to the left and the right, and just ahead was a living room that was open to the kitchen.

Garrett pointed to the right. "The master bedroom, music room, and library are that way. Dad's office and the other bedroom suites are to the left."

We continued into the living room. Nestled beyond the kitchen was an eating area surrounded by windows. The entire great room had windows along the back of the house that faced the patio and pool.

He nodded toward a door at the far end of the living room. "That leads to a game room and then to the dining hall. They have a dining room and kitchen in here, but in that space, it's easier to fit everyone. There is another kitchen out there too." He pulled open french doors. "This is the pool. Over there just outside the master bedroom is the hot tub."

"This is a beautiful home."

"What do you like about it?" He ushered me back inside and out of the cold.

I found his question surprising, and I took a second to think about what I loved about the place. "I love the wide-open floorplan. The high ceilings, the stone and tile." Walking along the island, I ran my hand along the granite countertop. "And I love this island. The whole kitchen really."

He smiled down at me. "I'm glad you like it. Let's head over to the dining hall." He pushed open the door he'd pointed to earlier. "Dad added the game room so the ranch hands would have a place to hang out. They have small cabins, similar to mine, located just over the hill behind the house."

Before following him into the game room, I stopped and admired the Christmas tree. "Lilith has great taste. I'm assuming she did this."

"Yeah. Left to dad, it would have been covered in lots of lights and strands of popcorn. He goes nuts for Christmas. Lilith has the decorating skill."

I followed Garrett through the game room and into the dining hall.

Ava rushed toward me, wiping her hands on her apron. "It's good to see you." She wrapped her arms around me and squeezed. "Thank you for taking care of Garrett. I'm a little put out that he didn't tell me what happened earlier, but it sounds like he was in good hands."

"He didn't want y'all to worry. He looked pretty roughed up for the first few days." I extended my hand as Lilith walked up. "Hi, I'm Tessa. I've seen you around, but I'm not sure we've ever officially met."

Lilith pulled me into a hug. "Ditto to what Ava said. And it's nice to meet you too. I think you've met Beau, Mad Dog, Clint, and Joji already."

"I have. It's nice to see you."

Beau nodded. "I owe you. If you ever need anything, let me know."

"You don't owe me." I glanced at the door as the ranch hands filed in. "Parker!"

A wide grin spread across Parker's face. "I didn't know you ever left the doughnut shop."

"Whatever." I hugged him. "How's your sister? She moved to…" I couldn't remember, so I left the sentence unfinished, hoping Parker would tell me where.

"Fort Worth. She's good. Has kids now." He rolled his eyes.

I rested a hand on Garrett's arm. "In high school, Parker's sister and I were friends, and he used to be such a little brother and tagalong all the time."

Parker shrugged. "It got me all kinds of attention from the older girls. 'Go away, Parker.' 'No, Parker, I won't go with you to the school dance.' 'Here, Parker. Carry this. If you are going to hang around, at least be useful.' Lots of attention." Chuckling, he dropped into a chair. "Fun times."

One by one, I met all the ranch hands, and then Garrett and I sat down. Set out on the table were bowls of guacamole, a platter of grilled onions and peppers, and bowls of shredded cheese. Tortilla warmers were clustered at each end of the table.

Beau walked in carrying a platter piled high with beef and chicken fajitas. My mouth watered. This was a rare treat.

During dinner, no one screamed at each other, which confirmed that I'd made the right choice about Christmas. His family was nothing like mine. Or at least like mine used to be. Time would tell if the attempt at getting along would last.

Garrett laughed and joked with the others around the table. His worries about being seen as an outsider were unfounded. He belonged here.

And thanks to everyone, I felt like I did too... just because I was Garrett's friend.

* * *

As we walked up to my car, Garrett stuffed his hands in his pockets. "I hope you enjoyed dinner."

"I did, and now I'm even more excited about Christmas."

"Good. Hard to believe it's only two weeks away." He kicked at a rock.

"I know." I wasn't ready to leave. "How are your bruises? Healing okay?"

"I guess. I can only see half of them."

"Are you using the cream?"

He lifted his shoulders. "Where I can reach."

"Garrett, it will help. You should—" The words lodged in my throat when my brain figured out the puzzle. "Do you need help with that?"

"I wasn't going to ask, but yeah." He glanced at my car. "Why don't you ride with me to my cabin. I'll drive you back here after."

"Perfect." I followed him to his truck, and he helped me in.

The drive to the cabin was short, but I used every second to give myself a pep talk, reminding myself I'd rubbed cream on him before and there was nothing to feel weird about.

All those encouragements lasted until we walked into his cabin and Garrett reached for the buttons on his shirt. The world slowed to half speed, maybe slower than that, and I embarrassed myself by staring. The whole time.

Sweetheart that he was, Garrett acted like he didn't notice, but I knew he'd noticed because of his spy gene.

"Where do you want me?"

That was a loaded question.

"You don't fit on the couch, so I guess your bed."

He strolled into his room. "Excuse the mess." After picking up the cream, he sat on the edge of the bed. "If this is too awkward, I'm sure I'll live."

"Lie down."

He stretched out, and I rubbed my way down his back. "They are healing. Some have faded a lot. Is that all you need me to get?"

He nodded and grabbed a T-shirt and yanked it over his head. "It's getting close to your bedtime. I should drive you back to your car."

"Let me just wash my hands." After getting the cream residue off my hands, I rested a hand on his chest. "Garrett, if you need me, call. Okay?"

He squeezed my hand. "I'll remember that."

We drove back to the main house, and he ran around to help me out. "The cabin next to mine will be ready for you at Christmas. I know you don't live far away, but I thought you might want to be here early Christmas morning. That's easier if you stay on the ranch."

"I'm excited about staying in the cabin. I love it out here."

I crossed my arms, a little nervous about what I wanted to ask. Asking here was easier than asking when Garrett was shirtless in his cabin. "I'm going out to visit my parents next weekend, and I wondered if you'd like to come along. You've already been warned about the arguing, but if that doesn't bother you too much, I'd like for you to meet them. And Mom says they are trying not to argue as much." Even though I considered Garrett nothing more than a good friend, I wanted him to meet my parents. Introducing him would earn me hours of having to deny there was anything more than friendship between us, but I didn't care.

"Absolutely, I'd love to. What night?"

"Saturday."

"That'll be fun. And Eli mentioned that you usually have Christmas Eve dinner at his house. He invited me to join y'all." He crinkled his nose. "If you don't mind."

"Of course I don't mind. You'll love his mom. And his dad. They are awesome." I stepped closer and hugged him. "This was fun. Thanks for inviting me."

"Anytime, Tessa. You're one of the family now." He opened my door. "Will you let me know when you get home?"

"Sure." Since getting back from our vacation, we'd texted or talked every night. It seemed only natural to talk to him at the end of the day.

CHAPTER 14

I glanced at the time before calling my mom to remind her one more time that Garrett was only a friend. There was a small—make that huge—worry they'd embarrass me by talking about him as if he were my boyfriend.

With Garrett as a friend, I was happier. And no matter how shocking it seemed to some—ahem, Delaney—two people could be friends and spend time together without being in a romantic relationship.

"Mom, hi. Garrett will be here in a minute to pick me up, but I wanted to remind you that he is a *friend*. F R I E N D. We are not dating. Okay?"

"You said that, Tessa."

"I know, but please don't forget."

"What I don't understand is why you won't date anyone. I'm never going to be a grandma if you keep up with this stubbornness. Skeeter wasn't worth giving up on a *lifetime of happiness.*"

My mom was one person I didn't want advice from about a lifetime of happiness.

"I don't want to talk about Skeeter. Just please don't embarrass me today."

"Tessa dear, you know we'd never do that." My mom's chuckle did nothing to reassure me.

"He's here. Bye." I ran to the door, trying to school my features so Garrett wouldn't read my frustration. "Hey. Come in. I just need to grab the gifts."

Garrett stepped inside, his hands shoved deep in his pockets. "Want help?"

"Sure." I held out the small stack of gifts and waited as he pulled his hands out of his pockets.

The last few times we'd seen each other, he'd done that a lot—shoving his hands in his pockets.

He loaded them in the truck while I locked up, and when I walked up to the truck, he opened my door. "I wasn't sure what to get your parents, so I bought them a digital frame that has *My Pets* written on the front, and I also got them a fuzzy blanket with cats all over it. Think they'll like that?"

"You bought gifts for my parents?"

His brow lifted, creating creases in his brow. "Is that okay?"

"They'll love those. That's very sweet." I climbed into the truck, touched by his gesture.

It was good that I'd called Mom that one extra time.

* * *

WE'D BEEN AT MY PARENTS' house for over an hour, and no one had even raised their voice. Mom and Dad were on their best behavior with Garrett here, and it made the day enjoyable. I credited Garrett's presence because I still wasn't ready to believe things were changing with them.

"Garrett, why don't you ride with me to get some ice?" Dad stood and fished keys out of his pocket.

Garrett moved a cat out of his lap. "Sure." He glanced at me. "I'll be back."

Panicking inside, I nodded, acting like it was the most natural thing in the world for my dad to decide he needed ice right before dinner was going to be served. "See you in a bit."

They walked out the front door, and I ran to the kitchen. "Mom, what is Dad doing?"

"Getting ice." She didn't look up from the cutting board.

"He doesn't need Garrett for that."

She rested the knife across the board and met my gaze. "Dad wants to make sure *your friend* is well intentioned."

I rubbed my temples. "What part of my begging wasn't clear? We aren't dating."

"Yet." Mom added the vegetables into the salad and tossed it all together. "He seems very nice."

"He *is* nice." And I didn't want my parents to scare Garrett away. I walked out to the back porch, hoping Dad wasn't making the run for ice too uncomfortable for Garrett. If I'd known my parents were going to behave like this, I wouldn't have brought him along.

Pacing, I checked the time every two minutes. How long could it possibly take to drive to the corner store and buy ice?

My stress melted away when Garrett stepped outside. "Aren't you cold out here?"

"I'm so sorry. I explained to my parents that we are just friends, but..." I shrugged. "Did he give you a hard time?"

"It was fine. We just talked. A bit of good news, I think maybe I talked him out of getting you a kitten." Garrett rested his hand on the small of my back. "Let's go back inside. Dinner's ready."

"I owe you for that."

"I'll keep that in mind." He pushed open the door.

My parents were already seated at the table. Garrett

pulled out my chair and waited for me to sit before lowering himself into the chair next to me.

Mom passed the salad to me, kicking off the meal.

As Dad doused his salad in ranch dressing, he asked, "Garrett, what do you do?"

"I'm currently between jobs. Previously I was working as a private investigator, but I'm hoping to move into ranching." Garrett worded it so he didn't sound like the spoiled kid who would inherit thousands of acres.

He wasn't a spoiled kid. He wanted to earn the spot beside his dad. I admired that about Garrett.

The rest of the afternoon went smoothly... until Coco pulled the leftover ham off the counter. There was a bit of yelling, but most of it was directed at the dog.

I tried to use that as an excuse to make an exit, but Mom insisted on opening gifts before we left, so we all settled in the living room. I'd be cleaning cat hair and dog hair off my clothes for a week or more.

I received the expected pajamas. They gave me a new pair every year. They loved what Garrett had bought them, and Mom had pictures loaded on the digital frame within minutes.

When Dad handed Garrett a small box, I held my breath.

He unwrapped the box, and a grin lit his whole face. He held up the mug with the word *Friend* emblazoned on the side. "Thanks. This is great."

My parents thought they were comedians. After tonight, Garrett might retract his Christmas invitation. Even if he didn't, he'd likely never come with me to see my parents ever again, and I couldn't blame him.

After helping Mom shove all the wrapping paper into a trash bag, I checked the time.

"I should get you home. You have to be up early to make doughnuts." Garrett stood and extended his hand to my dad.

"It was nice to meet you, sir." Turning to my mom, Garrett continued being his charming self. "Mrs. Best, thank you for dinner. I've had a wonderful time."

Mom hugged him. "You're welcome any time. Even if Tessa is busy."

He chuckled and ushered me out the door.

When we were finally closed into the truck, I breathed a sigh of relief. "Thanks for coming today, and I'm sorry if my dad grilled you."

"I enjoyed today."

"Shockingly, my parents didn't fight. Not once." I shifted in my seat to look at Garrett.

"About that…" He shot me a quick glance, then focused on the road. "Your dad mentioned that they started going to marriage counseling in September. I'm not quite sure why he decided to tell me, but I figured you'd want to know."

"I'm stunned. And happy, but really stunned. Although that fits with what Mom said the other day about trying." I tapped out a text to Mom, letting her know Garrett and I had both enjoyed the visit.

Whatever they were doing seemed to be working. They hadn't bickered or yelled at all today. Except at Coco, and she deserved it.

I thought back through the day and remembered the way Mom had smiled at Dad when he'd patted her hip in the kitchen. Public displays of affection weren't common with them. Maybe they'd achieve marital bliss after all.

"Hearing that news makes little things that happened today stand out. They seem happier. I never thought they'd be happily married. Ever."

Garrett smiled. "I'm glad to see them happy."

"When are you going to talk to your dad? After you said you were thinking about moving into ranching, it's been on my mind."

"Sundays on the ranch are usually fairly quiet. So I'm planning to talk to him tomorrow." He flashed a smile. "But I'm a little... nervous isn't quite the right word."

"That is going to be an early Christmas present for him. He is going to be so happy."

"I think so. I *hope* so." Garrett rolled his shoulders. "I'll let you know how the conversation goes."

"Thank you. If you aren't busy, we could meet up after the shop closes. I really do want to hear how he reacts."

He nodded. "That'd be great. I found a spot on the ranch I want to show you. Maybe we can walk tomorrow."

"Perfect." I tilted my head back, my eyelids drooping as it neared my bedtime. "Today was a good day. Tomorrow will be too."

I stared at Garrett's profile, appreciative of our friendship. But I also felt a little guilty. Although I was stubborn, I wasn't stupid. If I changed my mind about dating, Garrett would ask me out in a heartbeat. I knew that.

Was it wrong to like things as they were? This was comfortable. And he wasn't trapped. Our friendship would just change when he found someone who was open to romantic relationships. And when that happened, I wouldn't... have any right to be upset.

CHAPTER 15

*A*n hour before closing, I smiled as Beau walked into the shop. I opted to keep quiet about Garrett and ranching because I wasn't sure if that conversation had taken place yet.

"Good afternoon, Mr. Henry. What can I get you today?"

He surveyed the glass case. "We'll get to what I want in a minute. First, I want to thank you."

"I didn't mind helping Garrett. I enjoyed getting to know him better. He's kind and funny. You must be very proud of him." I couldn't imagine any dad not being proud of a man like Garrett.

"I am. But that thank-you wasn't for taking care of him. It was for whatever you said that changed his mind. He wants to learn about ranching. My son will someday step into my boots, as it were, and that makes me very happy."

I felt happy tears coming on. "I can't take credit for that, but I'm very pleased that he's going into the family business."

Beau leaned on the counter. "Can't take credit? Garrett said you were the one who made him see that he was letting fear get in the way. I will forever be grateful." He rubbed his hands together. "As for what I want. I'll take everything you have left."

For a Sunday, it had been slow, and I had dozens and dozens of doughnuts left.

"You don't have to..." I twisted the corner of the apron around my finger. "I can't let you do that. There is too much here."

"Too much? You've met the ranch hands. They can devour a dozen doughnuts faster than our bull Houdini can escape a pasture. And just so you won't worry about those guys getting too much sugar, I'll drop some off with the firemen on my way home." He crossed his arms. "Will it cause you trouble if you sell out before closing?"

"No. It happens occasionally. I just put up a sign that says I've sold out."

"Well, make that sign." He pulled out his wallet. "You can get out of here an hour early and go do something fun."

"Thank you." I packed up the doughnuts and rang up the total, wondering if Beau had any idea that the something-fun I'd planned was with his son.

Beau carried the doughnuts out in multiple loads. "What do you normally do with what's left at the end of the day?"

"Most days, I take what's left to the firemen. On Saturdays, I set them aside to take to church the next day." I picked up the last two bags. "I'll help you carry these out."

"Thanks." After everything was loaded, Beau tipped his hat. "See you later."

I waved, then ran inside and sent a text to Garrett. *I sold out early thanks to your dad. I'm going to clean up a little, but I can meet you out there in thirty minutes.*

He replied right away. *Great. I'll meet you at the main house.*

After putting up a sign, I raced through the shop, getting it ready for tomorrow morning as quickly as possible because I wanted to hurry out to the ranch... to Garrett. It was easy to admit how excited I was when my heart wasn't being risked. We were friends who enjoyed spending time together. I was happy with how things were, and one day if—more likely when—he met someone who sparked romance in his life, I'd step back and let him find his happily ever after.

I couldn't pretend that wouldn't hurt, but I could avoid thinking about it.

My phone buzzed as I hung up my apron.

Bring your swimsuit, and we can soak in the hot tub. Garrett sent a happy face emoji. *That'll warm us up after we walk.*

I sent a thumbs-up. While I liked the plan, I definitely wouldn't be snuggling with him in a hot tub where anyone and everyone could walk by and see. People would get the wrong impression.

* * *

WHEN I JUMPED out of the car, a dog trotted up to me. Instead of jumping up and trying to lick my face, this dog sat, patiently waiting to be scratched. "Hi there. Aren't you a good dog? What's your name?"

"That's Blue." Garrett squatted beside the dog and gave him a good rub. "He is a great dog. His one flaw is that he doesn't like other dogs around, but he does tolerate the cats."

"He seems sweet. Maybe if I'd grown up with a dog like this, I'd feel differently about man's best friend."

Garrett laughed, and I realized what I'd said.

"No pun intended." I shifted the bag on my shoulder. "I can't wait to see more of the ranch."

"Great. I'll put your bag in the guest room, and then we'll go. Mind if Blue tags along?" He tucked my bag under his arm. "Want to come in?"

"I'll wait out here." I knelt in front of Blue. "You aren't so bad. I think we'll be good friends."

Parker walked around the corner of the house, a doughnut in each hand. "Hey, Tessa. I'm seeing you out here a lot. Is that because you and Garrett are—"

"Friends." I finished the sentence to eliminate any confusion.

"That is exactly *not* what I was going to say, but I'll remember that." After taking a bite of a doughnut, he grinned. "Y'all have fun. And these doughnuts are the *best*." Chuckling, he walked toward his truck. "Catch you later, Tessa."

"Bye, Parker." I jumped when a hand touched my shoulder. "Oh, Garrett. I didn't even hear you walk out of the house."

"I can be vewy vewy quiet." Garrett winked then dropped the tailgate on his truck. "Hop up, Blue."

The dog obeyed, his tail wagging.

"How far away is it?" I buckled into my seat.

"Not too far, but the walk is partially uphill, so I want to conserve energy for that." He pulled away from the house, and not long after we passed the ranch hands' cabins, he turned and left the road completely.

We drove through a field of flowering weeds and along a line of trees. After a mile or more, he stopped.

"See the hill beyond these trees? That's where we're headed." He grabbed a backpack out of the back seat. "I brought water."

"This ranch is so big. It's a wonder people don't get lost." I petted Blue as he eased up beside me.

"I'm still learning my way around. Just wait until we get up the hill. You can see the entire ranch." Garrett headed into the trees.

I stayed beside him. "You haven't said how the conversation went."

"Right. Yeah. It went really well. Dad was even more

excited than I imagined." Garrett draped an arm around me without breaking his stride. "And I might've let your name drop as part of the reason."

"I found that out when your dad bought all the doughnuts I had left. I felt so bad because you were the one who made the decision. It wasn't me."

Garrett dropped his arm. "You were more of a help than you know. And the guys all loved the doughnuts. I might've stashed a couple extra aside to eat late tonight when I get a sugar craving."

When we reached a narrow part of the trail, I stepped behind him and put a hand on his back. He reached behind him, and I shifted my hand into his. When the path widened and we were side by side again, I kept my hand where it was. Conversation quieted as we made our way up the hill. Halfway up, I stopped to pull off my hoodie.

"You okay? Need some water?" Garrett stepped closer to me.

I let go of his hand only long enough to take off my hoodie and tie it around my waist. "I'm good. It's just too warm for that hoodie right now."

He helped me over some rocks, and after thirty minutes of hiking, he squeezed my hand as we reached the top of the hill.

"This view is amazing!" I turned in a circle. "From up here, you can see for miles."

"It's pretty great. Dad's house sits up high, but this spot has an even better view." Garrett handed me a bottle of water. "I hiked up here the other day, and I couldn't wait to show you."

He yanked a bowl out of his backpack and poured water into it. Blue lapped it up.

"Can you imagine being out here at night? Instead of seeing city lights, you'd be wrapped in a blanket of stars." I stepped closer to Garrett. "So those are the cabins we passed on the way up here, right?"

Standing with his shoulder touching mine, he pointed. "Yep. And if you look over there, that's the goat farm. The main house is over there, and somewhere in that cluster of trees is my cabin."

I walked to the other side of the plateau at the top of the hill. "This is amazing. I think I said that already."

"One of the things Dad said when we talked was that he wants me to pick a place to build a house so that this ranch feels like home. And while I like my cabin, building a house has a sense of permanence to it." He shoved his hands in his pockets. "I made another decision too."

"What's that?"

"The Henry family has owned Stargazer Springs Ranch for generations. And I think it's only *right* that if I'm going to follow in my dad's footsteps, I should be a Henry."

"Changing your name is a big deal." I stepped closer to him. "But if life hadn't pulled you away from your dad, you'd have grown up as Garrett Henry."

"True. I started the process last week. I'm hoping it will be completed by Christmas. Please don't say anything."

"Of course not." I was fairly certain I wouldn't have to dodge questions about Garrett changing his name. I rubbed his arm. "If you can figure out how to get a road to here, this would be the perfect spot for a house. You could have a rooftop patio."

He stared at the horizon. "And a hot tub."

Suddenly I was jealous of some unknown woman, the one who would enjoy forever with Garrett.

Crossing my arms, I tried to smile. "What about a hot tub on the rooftop patio?" I got the words out without choking up.

Blue nudged my leg, giving me the perfect excuse to bury

my face in his fur. If a dog could tell that I was upset, it probably wasn't a secret to Garrett either, but to his credit, he emptied the dog bowl and pretended I was just giving Blue attention.

"This will be a beautiful spot for a house." I pulled my hoodie back on.

"We'll see. I may end up building something closer to the main gate. Not sure yet." He stuffed the bowl back into the backpack. "You ready to head back down?"

Acting like nothing was wrong when I was visibly upset was silly. Garrett and I were friends.

"I'm not upset with you, Garrett."

He tugged me into a hug. "I know." He held onto me and rested his chin on my head. "Have I mentioned that I don't like Mosquito Boy?"

Laughing, I pulled away. "You've been talking to Eli."

"How can you tell?" His blue eyes twinkled.

"Would you be upset if I didn't stay for a soak in the hot tub?" I had some deep thinking to do, and the only thinking I'd do in a hot tub with Garrett would be indulging every sort of persuasion for why it didn't matter that we spent so much time together and claimed we were only friends.

Looking down at me, he wiped a tear off my cheek. "I don't mind, but I don't like to see you upset. I'm not sure exactly what is bothering you. I have only a general idea. But when I said I didn't expect anything from you, I meant every word. I don't care what your parents think or what Parker thinks. I care what you think."

Nodding, I whispered, "I don't know what I think."

His smile wasn't what I expected, but it calmed me.

"We're still friends?" The tease in his voice lightened the mood.

"Yes. And I'm still staying at the cabin for Christmas. Just promise me…" I wasn't sure I could get the words out, but they needed to be said.

"What's that?"

I inhaled, thinking through the words so that they wouldn't come out jumbled. "When you meet someone— someone you'd want to date—promise me that you won't let the opportunity go." As much as it would sting to see him with someone else, I wanted him to be happy… and not alone.

He needed someone who could make him happy day… and night.

Garrett stared at the landscape and rubbed the scruff on his jaw. After a second, he met my gaze. "I promise that when I meet someone who captures my heart, I will expend every last ounce of my energy to capture hers." His eyebrows lifted. "Does that make you feel better?"

"Yes." I could enjoy our friendship, knowing that he'd move on when he found a special someone. Now, I didn't have to think about it anymore.

"Since I don't expect to meet anyone new in the next three weeks, I was hoping you'd be my plus one for Eli's wedding." He flashed a smile that somehow made sunlight dance in his eyes. "Just friends."

"Sure. But if you do meet someone, tell me."

"I'll keep you completely updated on my love life." The tease was back in his voice.

Blue barked.

"Garrett is funny, isn't he?"

There hadn't been any great revelations, but I felt better about our friendship. I loved being friends with Garrett, and if he was comfortable with how things were, no other opinion mattered.

We started back down the hill toward the truck, and

when I tried to imagine how Garrett would look in a suit, I almost tripped.

He reached back and grabbed my hand. "Careful."

All thoughts of Garrett in a suit needed to be saved for when I wasn't in danger of rolling down a hill.

CHAPTER 16

*M*y plan to go home and think was derailed the moment I saw Delaney's number on my screen. With only three weeks until the wedding, her nerves were starting to frazzle.

"Hey there." I wanted to be the voice of calm for my friend.

"Please tell me you aren't busy. Can you come over?" Her voice sounded strained, but at least it didn't sound like she'd been crying.

"I can be there in two minutes. I just finished hiking with Garrett."

"Oh good. Do you know the way through the back gate?"

I waved to catch Garrett's attention. "I'll find out. Be there soon."

He leaned down to my window. "What's up?"

"What's the fastest way to the goat farm? Delaney is having a mini crisis, I think."

He pointed, giving directions and mentioning landmarks. The man knew how I navigated.

"Thank you." I started the engine. "I had a lot of fun today.

And I'm glad you showed me that spot. A house up there would be amazing."

He smiled. "Good. I'll talk to you later. Call me when you get home."

"I will." I followed his directions and parked in front of the trailer a few minutes later.

Delaney waited on the porch. "Thank you so much for coming. I'm having trouble with the seating arrangements. I've stared at it for so long, and Eli isn't much help. He says people will be happy with whatever. The only thing he said was not to sit Tandy and his granddad anywhere near each other."

"Yeah. Don't do that." I followed her inside.

"In a minute you have to tell me why. Eli won't talk about it." She sat down at the table and ran a hand over a seating chart before wiping her eyes. "And thanks to Eli and Garrett, I contacted my mom. She's coming."

"Oh, Delaney! That's wonderful." I hugged her.

I'd been so wrapped up with Garrett's injuries and healing, I hadn't even thought of what I shouldn't say to Delaney about Eli and Garrett meeting at the doughnut shop. But now, she knew that Eli had hired Garrett, and I didn't have any secrets to keep.

"I'm so happy Garrett found her. He's great at the private investigator stuff." Her smile left no question about how she felt.

"Funny you should say that because he's getting out of it. He's going to be a rancher."

"I'm sure his dad is happy about that."

"He is. But tell me more about your mom."

Delaney grinned. "She sounds like she's doing well. Not perfect, but better than the last time I talked to her. And I think she hadn't reached out because she wasn't sure if I wanted contact."

"It's great that you found her." I sat down, and seeing the tears in Delaney's eyes, I steered the conversation in a more productive direction. "Now, let's figure this out."

She pointed at a small table on the chart. "Instead of having a head table for all the wedding party, this table is just for me and Eli. I'm letting everyone else sit at the other tables. Eli has Zach and Harper as groomsmen, and I have you and Cami. Zach will want to sit with Haley, and I was going to seat you next to Garrett because y'all are friends."

"Perfect. Garrett and I are attending together." I saw Delaney's facial muscles twitch and quickly added, "As friends."

She clasped my hand. "I'm not saying that it's a bad idea for you to be friends with Garrett, but what's going to happen if a woman sweeps in and steals him away?"

I'd thought about that many times, and I knew the answer. When Garrett found the love of his life, I'd pull away and nurse a broken heart, but that would be easier than being a disappointment. I told people I wasn't willing to risk my heart. That was partially true. But ultimately, I wasn't willing to risk being not enough. That truth had been buried in the story I told Garrett, but I'm not sure he completely understood. As much as I loved and trusted Delaney, I couldn't tell her that part of my story.

I blew out a breath. "Let's just work on the seating chart."

"It can wait a few minutes. Talk to me." Delaney walked into the kitchen and pulled out hot chocolate packets. "With or without marshmallows?"

"With. Always." I crossed my arms on the table and laid my head down. "I don't want to think about Garrett with someone else. But I care for him too much to want him to stay single because of me. This topic came up today on our hike."

She set two mugs on the table and slid the bag of marshmallows toward me. "And?"

"I made him promise that he wouldn't ignore an opportunity." I poured in marshmallows until the chocolate could no longer be seen.

Delaney added only a few to her mug. "How did he respond?"

"He said that when he found the right woman, he'd expend all his energy to win her heart." I sipped my chocolate, getting a mouthful of marshmallows in the process. "And when that happens, I'm going to need you to take the doughnuts away from me."

She laughed.

Wiping tears, I shook my head. "I'm pouring my heart out, and you're laughing."

"First of all, you make doughnuts for a living. How am I going to take them away from you? You'd only make more."

"True."

"And secondly, I can't imagine Garrett chasing *anyone else* anytime soon." Delaney stirred the marshmallows into her chocolate. "No matter what, I'll be here. Even if it means slapping doughnuts out of your hands."

The words "anyone else" played in my head, and I thought back to Garrett's carefully worded promise. He hadn't promised to date some unknown woman who might be part of his future. When he made that promise to pull out all the stops, he meant me. The realization made me giddy... for a half second, and then the panic crept in. I couldn't think about this now. If things went south and I spent three weeks eating doughnuts, I wouldn't fit into my dress. I wouldn't do that to Delaney and Eli.

"We haven't gone a single day without texting or talking since Thanksgiving. I look forward to spending time with him, but I'm *terrified* of labeling our friendship as anything else. I can't." I swirled the marshmallows around in my mug. "Dating him would risk having my heart broken, and I can't do that. I think I'll leave things as they are until the wedding —because I already said yes to being his plus one—and then I'll pull back a little so that he has space to find someone else. But thinking about it too much right now isn't a good idea."

Delaney set her mug down and looked me in the eye. "When I was being stupid, you called me out on that because you are my best friend. Now I'm returning the favor. That is the absolute worst plan." She tapped her fingernail on the table. "If you are afraid of having your heart broken, avoiding the label of dating isn't going to prevent that."

I swallowed down the rest of my chocolate. "Right, but I don't have the bandwidth for this right now. I need to think about Christmas and making cakes for your wedding, and…"

"Just enjoy his company. Don't worry about labels or giving him space. He's a grown man. If he needs space, he'll say so."

"And if he wants more than friendship?" I knew he did. Why was I asking Delaney this question? It would lead right into the conversation I didn't want to have.

"He'll show you." She smiled. "Now, seating. I need to know why Tandy can't be by Matthew."

"No one talks about it, so I don't know exactly. But they never speak to each other. I've only seen them in the same room a couple of times. But you can sit Matthew over here with Eli's parents. And Tandy knows Lilith, so you can sit her with the Henrys."

"Okay." She scribbled on the chart. "Now for the big question. What about my parents?"

"Tables for six or eight?" I scanned the page.

"Six. Should I have chosen eight? That just seemed so big." Her brow furrowed. "I'm second-guessing every single thing about this wedding."

"Eli?"

Delaney's face flushed as she smiled. "I'm a hundred percent sure about that part."

"Good. So, you could put Beau, Lilith, Joji, Clint, Tandy, and your mom at this table. They would keep your mom entertained and make her feel welcome. And then put your dad's family with Eli's parents."

"Then where would I put Matthew?"

"With Haley and Zach. Over here. Hank and Nacha and the baby are also at that table, so there is one extra chair."

"Perfect. And last question. Your parents?"

"With me and Garrett. And if you don't have Ava and Mad Dog assigned yet, put them at that same table."

Delaney hugged me. "Thank you. You've made this so easy."

"And thank you for being honest with me. I'm just going to table that entire line of thought until after you are Mrs. Gallagher. I can't believe the wedding is only three weeks away."

"I know. I'm so excited." She glanced out the window as a truck door slammed. "I say that Eli makes me happy, but that's not it really. I wasn't unhappy before. But with him, I'm more content, freer to be me. I know that sounds silly."

"It doesn't." The contented feeling was something I knew quite well. Recently.

The door swung open, and Sherlock bolted across the room as Eli entered.

"Hey, Eli."

"Oh no. Not the chart." He feigned horror.

Delaney kissed him. "Oh stop. We're done. Tessa helped me."

"Tessa, you're a lifesaver. Delaney kept asking me about where to seat people and then got upset when I said we should pin the chart to the wall and throw darts to decide." Eli chuckled. "I don't know why she didn't like my idea."

I leaned down as Sherlock sniffed my pants. "You smell Blue, don't you?"

Sherlock jumped and tried to lick my face.

"Sit."

He dropped to his haunches, his tail wagging.

"Good boy!" I petted him. "Y'all have really been training him."

Eli and Delaney blinked, and then she said, "We have. But why are you acting as if you like dogs all of a sudden?"

"Turns out, I sort of like well-behaved dogs." I picked up my purse. "I'm going to go, so that y'all can do couply things and I can eat and relax before going to bed."

Eli opened the front door. "Are you and Garrett coming for Christmas Eve dinner?"

"We are. I talked to your mom yesterday. She's so excited about having an extra mouth to feed." I laughed. "See y'all later."

I climbed into the car and drove home. When I walked back into my apartment, I texted Garrett. *I'm home.*

Thanks for letting me know. I'll see you in the morning.

Dang my heart for being so excited about that.

CHAPTER 17

I flipped the open sign, and a familiar hand reached for the handle as I turned the lock. "Good morning."

Garrett had been the first customer every day this week. The term customer wasn't accurate because I never charged him, but he always dropped a tip in the jar.

He grinned as I hugged him. "Good morning. Now that I'm going to be a rancher, I need to learn to be up with the sun. I'll be adopting your bedtime before too long."

"It's not so bad. Excited about the new job?" I hurried behind the counter and pulled his favorite out of the case.

"I am."

I slid a doughnut across the counter and set a mug next to it. "I won't get to see you in the mornings. You'll be eating Ava's breakfast and taking care of cows."

"I'll sneak over whenever I get a chance." He broke the doughnut in half. "Have you decided what days you'll be closed?"

"I plan to put a sign up today. Christmas Eve, I'll only be open until noon. Then I'll be closed for Christmas and the day after. I don't want to stay closed too long because I'm closing again for the wedding two weeks later." I filled a mug of coffee for myself. "I should probably hire extra help so that taking a break isn't such a big deal."

"That's wise. You'll exhaust yourself, trying to keep this place going all the time." He nodded toward the door as it opened. "I'm going to settle at that table in the corner while you feed the masses."

"Let me know if you need anything." I smiled as firemen filed in. "Good morning, guys. What can I get for y'all?"

An hour later, the crowd had thinned a bit, but Garrett still sat at the corner table. He seemed preoccupied with whatever he had laid out in front of him, and I chose not to interrupt him.

The steady stream of customers made it hard to make it over to his table anyway.

As I was getting a fresh pot of coffee ready to brew, the door opened. "I'll be with you in one moment."

"No hurry."

The familiar voice startled me, and I nearly dropped coffee grounds all over the floor.

With a forced smile, I turned and faced Deputy Gomez. "Hi."

Not only was this man a reminder of the awful beating Garrett had suffered, but I was also harboring irritation for the implications Nico had made during the visit at the house.

"Welcome to Sweet's. What can I get for you?"

He perched on a barstool not far from the coffee station. "I was out this way and thought a doughnut and coffee sounded good. Do you have any of that kind you made at the house?"

I tensed, hoping no one else heard his question. Out of context, it sounded like he'd been at my house. I didn't want people to think that.

After hitting the button to start the coffee brewing, I walked back behind the counter. "I make a batch of those every day." I pulled out a praline doughnut and slid it over to him. "Coffee will be ready in about five minutes." I set a to-go cup in front of him.

He needed to be able to take it with him when he left, which would hopefully be soon.

Nico took a bite and smiled. "Garrett was right. These are the best." He dusted crumbs off the front of his shirt, then looked at me. "I'm sorry about implying…" He waved a hand as if that completed the sentence.

"Apology accepted."

Garrett was on the phone, focused on papers laid out on his table. I wanted him to look up and notice who was here.

But while he finished up his call, I could gather a bit of information. "Have there been any more developments… in the case?"

Nico nodded. "Big developments. I drove out this way to talk to Garrett, but the woman I spoke to out there said he wasn't working on the ranch today. Know where I can find him?"

"Hang on." I ran over to Garrett's table and patted his arm once.

"Gotta go." His eyes wide, he smiled up at me. "What's up?"

I leaned close, then pointed behind me. "Nico showed up." I didn't even get a chance to tell Garrett about the big development before he was striding across the room.

"Nico, what a surprise." Garrett acted like they were old friends.

Nico motioned toward his doughnut. "Decided to have one of these when I didn't find you at the ranch, but it should've occurred to me to look for you here… since y'all are *friends*."

149

What was his deal? Garrett and I were the only ones who were allowed to emphasize that word when talking about our relationship.

"I'm here often." Garrett pointed toward his table. "We can sit over there and talk."

Nico pulled out his wallet. "How much do I owe you?"

I rang up his purchase, then swiped his card. "Y'all let me know if you need anything. And the coffee is probably ready."

They settled at the table, and I served other customers who walked in. Curiosity about what was being said at that corner table gnawed at me, but I couldn't ignore customers to go listen. I'd just have to wait until Garrett filled me in.

Fifteen grueling minutes later, Nico tipped his hat before walking out the door.

Garrett gathered his papers and strolled up to the counter. "You busy tonight?"

"Not if you are going to tell me what he said." How would I make it until dinner without knowing? "I can make something."

"Sounds good. Let me know what time." He glanced at his phone. "I need to run. Christmas presents don't wrap themselves."

"See you later." I'd have to figure out what to make for dinner, something impressive.

* * *

RATHER THAN TRYING to reinvent the wheel, I'd texted Ava to get her enchilada casserole recipe. And it smelled delicious bubbling in my oven.

Garrett knocked right on time, and I hurried to the door.

"Come in. Dinner is almost ready."

He sniffed the air as he walked inside. "That smells amazing. Almost like—" A smile spread across his face. "You made enchilada casserole."

"I did. Ava gave me the recipe." I hurried into the kitchen when the timer beeped. "I've been waiting all day to know what Nico told you."

Garrett leaned against the counter. "Good news. Well, to me it's good news. To the—what was it you took to calling her?"

"The she-devil."

"Yeah. To her, it's not good news."

I pulled off my oven mitts, waiting for him to spill the news. "Are you teasing me with silence on purpose?"

"Possibly." He rested his hands on my hips. "Nico couldn't give me all the details, but you no longer need to hire anyone for your case."

I pressed both hands to his chest. "Really?"

He glanced down, then inched me closer. "She's been arrested for trying to hire someone to kill her husband. I guess when getting him jailed didn't work, she changed up her plan. But then her husband threatened to kill his wife and took a swing at a deputy who was serving a search warrant. So, the guy who beat me up landed in jail too."

"Arrested? Both of them?" That was what I'd wanted to happen but more than I'd expected. I slid my arms around his neck. "That's great news."

His arms tightened around me, and he stayed quiet.

I pulled back but didn't step out of his embrace. "Isn't that good news?"

He nodded. "Very good news."

"But?"

Shaking his head, he pulled me close again. "No but. It's good news." He rested his chin on top of my head. "I'm grateful I'm around to hear the good news."

I stayed with my head resting against his chest. "She

called your phone all those times, thinking you were dead, didn't she? She was going to let her husband kill you and then report him." Even the thought made my insides ache.

Garrett kissed the top of my head. "Not sure. But thanks to you, that's not the way this played out."

With my face buried in his chest, I thought of the contented feeling Delaney mentioned. Before my brain ran away with that idea, I boxed it back up. My heart was definitely on the butchering slab, but I was going to pretend it wasn't until after the wedding.

"I'm happy about that." I rubbed the front of his shirt as I stepped back. "And I'm glad I'm the one who found you."

His silent smile said he agreed.

CHAPTER 18

earing jeans and a simple red sweater, I pulled up in front of the cabins just before one in the afternoon on Christmas Eve. To say that I was as excited as a kid at Christmas accurately depicted my emotions. Thanks to my friendship with Garrett, this ranch had started to feel like home.

Garrett waved from the porch of what would be my cabin for the next few days. I hoped my friendship with him would last a long time, and not just because he could fill out a pair of jeans better than any other man in this hemisphere. Would I still wish I hadn't made myself that promise if he'd been average-looking? Probably. What I liked most about Garrett was the way he made me feel, and his looks had little to do with that.

He opened my car door. "You planning to stay or just going to sit in the car for a while?"

"Merry Christmas!" I opted to pretend that I hadn't been staring at him. "I can't remember being this excited about Christmas since... forever." I hugged him.

"How were things at the shop this morning? I'm sorry I

didn't make it over there." He kept me close a few heartbeats longer than normal.

"It was busy. I was really glad I opened today. There wasn't much left, but I dropped off the last few dozen at the fire station."

He grabbed my bag from the back seat. "I know they appreciate that."

"Tessa, you made it!" Ava smiled as she climbed out of her truck, which I hadn't even heard pull up. "Would you be up for making Christmas cookies with us?"

"Sure." I glanced at Garrett. "Is that all right with you? We don't have to be anywhere until five."

"Absolutely fine by me. I'll take your bag inside if you want to ride over with Ava."

"Thanks." I buckled into the passenger seat and watched as Garrett waved before walking inside.

"He's a gem." Ava pressed a hand to her heart. "I'm so glad he found his way to the ranch. He belongs here."

"He is just as happy that he found all of you." I pulled a scrunchie out of my purse and tied my hair up. "What kind of cookies are we making?"

"Mexican wedding cookies, sugar cookies—I have cookie cutters in all sorts of shapes—and some peppermint chocolate chunk cookies. Most of the ranch hands go home for Christmas, but a few of them are from around here. I try to keep them all well fed." Christmas spirit emanated off her like an energy force. "For a couple, this is their home." She pointed at one of the houses up the hill. "Kent lives up there next to me. You've met his son, haven't you? I'm not sure who is most excited about Christmas this year—Beau or Mason."

"Garrett mentioned that Kent lived out here with his son. I know all the guys appreciate you. I've heard you do a wonderful job of not only keeping them fed, but happy as well."

Her eyes misted. "I want all of them to be happy. That's why I'm so glad you decided to spend Christmas here."

I nodded, not sure how to respond.

She hopped out of the truck and motioned for me to follow. "They're meeting us in the dining hall."

When we walked through the door, Lilith and Joji waved from the counter.

Then Joji ran over to greet me. "We were hoping you'd come bake with us. I can only stay for a bit because I have to get everything ready for tomorrow. I'm having a houseful."

Lilith laughed. "I got off easy this year. Ava's cooking for everyone who will be at my house."

"Thanks for inviting me." I accepted the apron Ava held out. "What should I do?"

"We have a batch of sugar cookies waiting to be decorated. Stars and Christmas trees. You can decorate those, or you can make dough for one of the other kinds." Ava tapped recipes lying on the counter.

"I'll decorate."

She motioned toward ingredients sitting out. "I'm guessing you have a good icing recipe. If not, there is one in this pile here."

"I have a great icing recipe." I found a bowl and what I needed before mixing up a batch.

While I colored small bowls of icing, Lilith, Joji, and Ava mixed cookie dough.

They chatted as they worked, and I enjoyed listening to their stories. Their friendship reminded me of my friendship with Delaney and Cami, and I smiled at the thought we'd still be friends years from now. Of that I had no doubt.

"You know how she met Beau, don't you?" Ava pointed at Lilith.

"I don't, actually." I added tiny strands of icing and colorful dots so that the trees looked like they were draped with lights.

"He picked her up off the side of the road."

I dropped the bag of icing. "He what?"

Lilith nodded. "Car trouble. Beau rescued me."

Ava bumped her shoulder against Lilith's. "That first night, I knew Beau and Lilith were meant for each other. I'd never seen Beau so happy. And I'd known him nearly all his life."

"Some things are just meant to be. Like me making his life difficult." Lilith leaned toward me, acting as if she were going to whisper. "I wasn't open to the idea of a relationship in the beginning, so I took my attraction out on Beau."

Ava nodded. "She did. Acted like she hated him."

"What else was I supposed to do? I'd sworn off men, and Beau was hotter than the afternoon sun in August." Lilith shook her rolling pin. "But then I wised up."

I could relate to those feelings. Not that I thought Beau was hot, but even a glance from his son made my heart go pitter patter. "What changed your mind?"

The ladies grinned at each other, then answered in unison. "Christmas lights and a ladder."

"What sort of trouble are y'all cooking up in here? Does someone need the lucky ladder?" Clint grinned as he walked toward the counter.

Joji spun around and wiped her hands on her apron. "Hey there, handsome. You ready to head back to the farm?"

He nodded. "I am."

She untied her apron and handed it to Ava. "Merry Christmas. I'll catch y'all later."

Clint scooped her up, and Joji laughed as they left the room.

Lilith nodded toward the door. "If you ask Joji what a

fifty-year-old woman is doing acting that way, you know what she'll tell you?"

"What's that?"

"Enjoying herself."

More laughter erupted.

Ava moved into Joji's spot and cut out more cookies. It was funny to see them so giddy.

She was busy asking Lilith about how the venue was doing when Mad Dog stepped into the room. With her back to the door, Ava didn't see him.

He put a finger to his lips and crept up behind her. When he slid his arms around her waist and kissed her neck, she squealed.

"Mad Dog!" She flushed pink.

"Who else would be greeting you that way?" He picked up a decorated Christmas tree. "Being Ava's husband makes me the official taste tester."

"What do you need, love?" She kissed his cheek, then went back to cutting out cookies.

"Just got back from Jeffrey's and wanted to see you. I'm headed home in a sec." He picked up another cookie. "These are good. But I probably shouldn't eat them all right now. See y'all later." Whistling, he strolled out of the room.

Lilith glanced back at the door as he left. "Since Ava ratted on me, I'll tell you about her. Instead of facing her attraction, she pretended they were only *friends*."

Ava rolled her eyes. "That was just as bad as your acting like you hated Beau."

My goal was not to think about my friendship with Garrett, and these ladies were not helping.

* * *

IT WAS after nine when we left the Gallaghers' house and almost ten when we parked in front of the cabins.

"That was fun." Garrett shut off the engine.

"Aunt Patsy is always a wonderful hostess. I'm glad you went with me."

He ran around and opened my door. "You're probably exhausted."

"All the excitement has me feeling more awake than expected. You want to come in for a bit?" I nodded toward the door.

"I'd like that for two reasons. One, I like spending time with you, and two, I'd like to give you your gift tonight." He studied my face. "If that's okay."

There was no discomfort in having him close. The way he looked at me sent a rush of desire through my veins, but that was attraction, and I was all too familiar with that emotion. It seemed so at home in my head, I considered giving it a decorating budget.

I reached up and straightened his collar. "Of course it's okay." I'd expected to exchange gifts with lots of other people around, but I liked his idea better. "I have yours too."

Garrett's hand bumped mine as we walked toward the stairs, and all the stories I'd heard earlier in the day flooded my mind. It was easy to see how happy the ladies were, but none of them had given me the formula for getting past my fear. I wasn't sure there was a cure for that.

We walked into the cabin, and I scanned the main room. "It looks a lot like your place. But I don't remember curtains across the back of your living room."

"Mine doesn't have those." He took my hand. "Close your eyes."

I did as he asked and let him lead me across the room. The curtains moved along the rod. Then a door opened.

"Some might think this is a strange gift, but I'm hoping

you like it. Obviously." He squeezed my hand. "You can open your eyes."

I opened them and gasped. "A hot tub!"

"I couldn't exactly set one up in the middle of your apartment, so it's here at this cabin whenever you want to use it." He pressed a key into my hand. "Merry Christmas, Tessa."

Privacy screens blocked the view of the cabins on each side, making the space feel as private as the hot tub at the house in San Antonio.

"You built all this for me?"

He shoved his hands in his pockets. "I did. I started working on plans for it while we were at the house. This was my side project."

My heart raced, and my chest tightened. What I'd gotten him didn't compare to this at all.

"Tessa?" He hesitantly pulled one hand out of his pocket.

I stepped closer to him, wanting to bury my face in his chest and knowing I shouldn't. "I don't know what to say."

"You could say that you hate it, and you want me to send it back. Or..." He inched closer. "You could say that you like it and invite me to join you for a *friendly* soak in the hot tub."

I latched onto the word friendly. That word would get me through the next two weeks. Part of me wanted that word to last forever.

"No one has ever given me such an amazingly thoughtful gift. I love it." I hugged him, and his other hand came out of his pocket in a fraction of a second. "Now I know why Delaney suggested I pack my swimsuit *just in case*."

Garrett grinned. "I wrangled a few elves to help with the surprise. Like Ava, who made sure you were away from the cabin this afternoon while I finished installing the screens."

I gave him another quick hug. "Go get your swimsuit on."

He strode toward the door.

"Wait!"

Alarm registered on his face. "What's wrong?"

"Nothing, but you need to open your gift. I almost forgot that part. It's in my bag."

He pointed toward the bedroom. "I put it in there."

I rushed into the room and found another gift on the bed. My name was on the tag. "What's this?"

"Another present." He leaned against the doorframe. "Open it, and you'll understand."

I tore off the paper but froze when I saw the logo of Delaney's store on the box. Just thinking about lingerie had Skeeter's words blaring in my head. Inching backward away from the bed, I bumped into Garrett.

He rested his hands on my shoulders. "You can trust me, Tessa."

I glanced back at him. "I know."

Trusting Garrett was instinctive. He wasn't like Skeeter. Garrett wasn't the type to cheat. That only made this harder. I found someone I could trust, and he was the last person in the world I wanted to disappoint.

Also, I wanted to believe Delaney wouldn't have set me up to be blindsided with something lacy or see-through.

"I'm glad you trust me." His voice was almost a whisper.

I pulled off the lid and lifted the white fuzzy robe out of the box. "This looks exactly like the one at the house." I buried my face in the soft fabric. "You thought of everything."

"A reminder of that week. And of our friendship."

I dropped the robe onto the bed and pulled his gift out of my bag. "I was going to put a bow on it tonight, but I guess it doesn't matter if there is a bow."

He tore away the green-and-red striped paper. "You bought me a cowboy hat."

"I had an elf help me guess the sizing."

He set it on his head. "It's perfect. And now I know why

the guys made a game of putting their hats on my head the other day. Clint's hat made me look like I was five."

"It looks good on you." That was the friendly way of saying that he looked hotter than a tater tot in a fryer.

"Thanks." His blue eyes twinkled. "I'll meet you back here in five minutes. Should I wear my hat?"

"While it makes you look like a cowboy, I'd hate for it to get wet."

"True. Wouldn't want to ruin it." He pulled me close. "Thank you. I love it."

I circled my arms around his waist and buried my head in his chest. "Merry Christmas, Garrett."

He rubbed my back. "Merry Christmas."

A short time later, we eased into the warm bubbly water, and I sat next to him rather than in his lap.

"I think I'm going to be over here a lot." I lifted my legs until my toes popped out of the water. "This feels incredible."

"I'm glad to hear it. And I know it's farther from the shop and that the kitchen here is smaller, but you can live here if you want." He stared at the bubbles. "You said you loved it here on the ranch."

"I'll think about that." I definitely wouldn't be making a decision on that before the wedding.

"No pressure." He bumped his feet against mine. "Whatever makes you happy."

I couldn't think about what made me happy right now. That was off-limits.

* * *

CHRISTMAS MORNING ARRIVED way too early. I'd spent a large chunk of the night trying not to think about what made me happy. And I'd failed. But today was a new day.

Without changing out of my jammies, I yanked on tennis

shoes and a coat. As I stepped out the front door, Garrett emerged from his cabin.

"Perfect timing." He wore cowboy boots and his hat with his flannel jammies, and it was a sight.

"If we are the only ones in jammies over there, I'm not going to laugh." I pulled my coat closed as he opened the door of the truck.

"I'll laugh, but that's not going to be the case. Dad said he was changing back into his when we left the barn just a bit ago." He ran around and slid in behind the wheel.

"You've already been up and working."

"I helped this morning since we are down a few ranch hands." He parked in front of the house. "But Christmas morning is pretty casual around here. We'll go change before we have Christmas dinner later this afternoon."

I followed Garrett into the main house, and Beau met us at the door.

"Hey." His voice was almost a whisper. "Look over there." He pointed into the eating area.

Blue lay on the floor, and a large cat hung over the side of a chair, flipping its tail in Blue's face.

"Princess cracks me up." Beau chuckled.

"Princess, I take it, is the cat and not a pet name for Lilith." I watched as Blue twitched his ear, his only recognition of the cat's presence.

Beau's chuckle morphed into a full laugh. "I wonder what would happen if I called her that."

Garrett shook his head as he kicked off his boots. "Lilith's cat is funny. She is some sort of exotic, and she acts like she can't stand Blue, but anytime that dog's inside, she is right by him, trying to get his attention."

Beau nodded. "Blue is mostly an outside dog, but it's cold. And it's Christmas. Also, don't let the ear twitch fool you.

He's thrilled to get her attention. He just acts like it's no big deal."

"What are y'all going on about?" Ava stepped inside.

"We were discussing Princess and Blue's complicated friendship." Beau moved out of the way. "Come on in. I made coffee. Lilith should be out in a minute."

We all gathered near the kitchen island, and coffee mugs were passed around.

"Once everyone gets here, we'll go sit by the tree." Ava shuffled around the kitchen in her slippers, turning on the oven and pulling food out of the fridge. "The breakfast casseroles should be done when we finish opening gifts."

While they talked in the kitchen, I wandered over to the Christmas tree. Laughter rang out behind me, and I was glad I'd chosen to be here... even if it made my friendship with Garrett even more complicated.

* * *

GROWING UP AN ONLY CHILD, Christmas was usually quiet. Not this house. Several ranch hands lounged in their jammies, including Kent, who had the cutest kid. I'd seen Mason in the doughnut shop with Ava before, but now the pieces all fit together.

People chatted in small clusters as we sipped coffee and waited until it was time to open gifts.

Mad Dog smiled as he followed his daughter inside. "Sorry we're late. Poppy's plane was delayed."

Mason, who had shown immense patience this morning, darted across the room and jumped into Poppy's arms. "Merry Christmas!"

This was one huge happy family. Being a part of something like this would be—I wasn't allowed to think about that. After sucking in a deep breath, I counted to five, hoping all the unallowed thoughts would swoosh out with the air when I exhaled.

My plan didn't work.

Garrett ran his knuckles down my arm. "Everything okay?"

"Yeah. I'm just… happy. With everyone here, it feels so festive. Like family."

He patted my leg. "I'm glad you're here."

Mason dragged Poppy and Mad Dog toward the Christmas tree. "Let's open gifts."

"Great idea." Poppy handed him a present. "Why don't you start?"

And with that, the gift giving began.

Watching the paper piling up near the tree and hearing the laughter made the day perfect.

When all the presents under the tree had been passed around, Lilith stuffed wrapping paper into a trash bag. "I think that's it."

Garrett stood. "I have one more. Let me grab it." He ran outside and returned seconds later. "Dad, this is for you." He handed Beau an envelope.

Beau's brow knitted as he lifted the flap and pulled out the single sheet of paper. His blue eyes misted as he read. When he looked up, he smiled and blinked away the tears. "You changed your name."

"You're my dad, and this is my home." Garrett wrapped his arms around Beau.

I wiped at tears as others gathered around Garrett, hugging him and patting him on the back. No one acted as if he were barging in where he wasn't wanted. And the permanence of changing his name was truly a gift to his dad. That was clear.

Beau stood up. "Breakfast is in just a few minutes." He

crossed the room and sat beside me. "Parker mentioned you like to ride."

"I do. It's been a while, but I love horseback riding."

"Good. Come with me." He tapped Garrett's arm. "You too. Let's head outside." Beau pointed at the door. "Lilith, I'll be back in a few minutes."

When we got outside, Beau climbed into the back seat of Garrett's truck. Following his lead, we got into the truck.

Garrett pulled away from the house and headed in a direction I hadn't been. Three minutes later, we stopped outside a barn. Beau hadn't told Garrett where to go, which had to mean that he was in on the surprise.

Beau opened my door after getting out. "I hope you're enjoying Christmas. It can get a bit crazy around here. In a good way. I love it. It's my favorite holiday."

"I'm loving every minute. And I'm thankful I could be here."

Smiling, Garrett slid open the barn door.

Beau walked up to a stall, and a speckled horse stuck its nose over the side. "Merry Christmas, Tessa. This is Sprinkles."

I must've blinked twenty times before the words registered. "You're giving me a horse?"

"Yes. I'll never forget what you've done for my family. You and Garrett are friends, but the way I see it, you're family." He stroked the horse's nose. "We'll keep her here and feed her."

With my arms wrapped around myself, I tried to swallow the lump in my throat.

He glanced at Garrett. "Does the quiet mean she likes it?"

Nodding, I hugged Beau. "I love her. And I can't wait to ride." I wiped my eyes as I backed up. "But the family part means the most. Thank you."

He rubbed my shoulder. "Good. I'm going to head back

on the Mule. Y'all take as long as you need." Blinking, he strode out of the barn.

Garrett wrapped his arms around me. "In case you haven't figured it out, everyone here on the ranch loves you."

I closed my eyes and let his words sink into my bones. "When I helped you, I wasn't trying to score points or…"

He leaned down to whisper in my ear. "I know, Tessa. You were just being you."

I kept my head against Garrett's chest, acknowledging what made me happy. He did.

"He bought me a horse!" I clenched Garrett's shirt in my fists. "Do you think we'll have time to ride today?" Sorely tempted to kiss Garrett, I stepped away from him and kissed my horse instead.

"We should eat first. Then we'll ride." He bumped my shoulder. "Have you ever gone horseback riding in your jammies?"

"I haven't. But there's a first time for everything."

CHAPTER 19

The week after Christmas was a blur of activity. Between running the shop and helping Delaney with last-minute details for the wedding, I barely had time to sleep, which meant I didn't have time for friendly soaks in the hot tub or horseback riding.

It was New Year's Eve, and I made sure everything was in place before unlocking the door. Today would likely be busy, and I'd made extra doughnuts in preparation. All that was left to do was taping up the signs that let people know I'd be closed tomorrow and all of next weekend. If I continued closing this often, I'd need to move into the cabin just to make ends meet.

After taping up a sign on the front window and another near the register, I flipped the bolt on the door.

A steady stream of customers, who were getting their sugar fix for today and buying for tomorrow, had my doughnuts completely gone by noon. I taped up another sign, letting people know I'd sold out, then drove to my apartment.

Since my breakup with Skeeter, I hadn't attended a New

Year's Eve party. I'd rung in every new year sound asleep. But tonight, there was a party at the venue, and I'd promised Delaney and Eli that I'd be there.

Garrett hadn't mentioned it, but I knew he'd be there too.

I flipped through my outfits, trying to decide what to wear. Cami had mentioned that there would be a live band, so jeans and boots were probably the best option. After laying out what I planned to wear, I crawled in bed for a nap. If there was any hope of my staying up until midnight, I needed sleep.

* * *

"You didn't have to give me a ride. I could've driven myself." I walked with Delaney and Eli toward the big gathering room at the venue.

"Now you can toast in the new year." Eli tucked an arm around Delaney's waist.

"You were afraid I wouldn't show up." I did appreciate that they'd gone to the effort of making sure I made it.

Delaney bounced her head up and down. "Yes. We wanted you to be here."

"And now I'm stuck." I was more nervous about tonight than I had any reason to be.

Eli stopped and faced me. "Whenever you want to leave, tell me. I'll drive you home. Even if it means leaving my fiancée just as the countdown nears zero. I will leave and take you wherever you want to go."

"I'm not going to interrupt your big moment of the night."

He shifted so that he stood between me and Delaney. "We don't want you to feel trapped. We want you to have fun."

Delaney kissed his cheek. "What he said."

"Thanks. Y'all go in. I'm going to ease into the room." I wanted to get my bearings before feeling bombarded.

The doughnut shop was often crowded, but that was my space, and it didn't feel the same as being here even if the room was filled with faces I recognized, people who came into the shop regularly.

Then I spotted Garrett.

The sound I made was either me gasping or my heart screeching to a stop.

Wearing jeans that fit him just right, black boots, a long-sleeved paisley shirt, and the hat I'd given him, he looked like reason enough to stay. Meeting my gaze across the room, he tipped his hat.

I wove my way through the crowd, and we met in the middle of the dance floor. A new song started as I walked up, and Garrett lifted his eyebrows.

In answer to his silent question, I rested my hand on his shoulder. He touched a hand to my waist, and warmth danced through me even before our boots started moving.

"I'm happy you came. I wasn't sure if you'd be awake." He moved us around the dance floor, maintaining a polite distance between us.

"Delaney made me promise, so I took a nap today. It helped that I sold out early." I questioned my sanity for not ignoring my fear. Dating Garrett could be amazing. But it could also leave me staring disappointment in the face.

The image of a younger me stuffing her face with doughnuts flashed in my head, and I remembered why Garrett and I were only friends.

We danced through several songs. Then he led me off the dance floor to a table in the corner.

Cami waved as we approached. "I wondered where y'all were. Isn't this great? I hope Lilith has a New Year's party every year."

Haley rubbed her belly. "I'm pretty sure we won't make it next year."

Zach nodded. "We may not even make it until midnight this year." He draped an arm over the back of Haley's chair and kissed the side of her head.

Harper laughed. "Hank and Nacha are here. Kids are no excuse."

"And I've thanked Clint and Aunt Joji a hundred times for babysitting. We won't stay too late, but it is nice to have a date night." Hank dipped Nacha and kissed her.

Grinning, she slid her hands around his neck. "They did offer to babysit all night."

Hank turned and tugged on her hand. "See y'all later."

The table erupted in laughter. Then Hank and Nacha dropped into seats on the other side of the table.

"We'll visit for a bit." He draped an arm around her.

My friends made being in love look easy and painless. And there was no question by the way their husbands looked at them that they were good at making them happy.

Garrett nodded toward the bar. "Can I get you anything?"

I wanted a drink, but I needed food. "Yes. A margarita would be wonderful. I'm going to run to the buffet. Want anything?"

"Food." He winked. "I'll meet you back here."

Weaving my way to the food, I took the long way to avoid the women who'd been in the shop the day Garrett had asked me out the very first time. I could never remember their names because, in my head, I thought of them as the hens, or if they weren't together—hen one, hen two. But they were always in the middle of gossip, and I preferred to avoid being gossiped about. The less contact I had with them the better.

With two plates in hand, I made my way down the line, loading up on what I wanted and on what I knew Garrett would like. I carried the plates back to the table, smiling as Garrett set our drinks down.

He reached out to take the plates. "Good timing." His gaze jumped to something near my shoulder.

Then I felt the tap. "Tessa, hi. It's great to see you here. I haven't seen you at a New Year's Eve party since... well, you know." She cupped her hand near her mouth and pretended to whisper. "Since you were dumped."

Hen one had been drinking.

"This party sounded fun."

She chewed her bottom lip. "Ashley said the two of you were just friends."

Instead of pretending I didn't know who she was talking about—which I was tempted to do—I swallowed and gave a tiny nod.

A wide smile spread across her face as her gaze shifted. Garrett was behind me. I could feel him, and if I'd had any doubt, her look confirmed it.

"Will you introduce me?" She licked her lips.

A Tolkien-style epic battle raged inside me. I did not want to introduce her, but what right did I have to make that choice? But even a good friend wouldn't introduce her. She'd had no interest in Garrett when she sat near him in the doughnut shop, but now that she knew who he was, she wanted to be introduced to Beau Henry's son. I just had to figure out how to say no without making it sound like I wanted Garrett for myself.

I wasn't sure how to do that.

Strong arms wrapped around me. "Hey. Our food is getting cold."

Maybe I did love Garrett.

"Hey, hen." Eli stuck his hand out as he walked up. "Have you met my fiancée?"

While Eli introduced Delaney, I spun around and dropped into my seat.

Garrett squeezed my hand. "If she asks again, the answer is no. I remember her from the shop. I need someone nice."

At the moment I didn't feel very nice.

Eli dropped into the chair next to me. "You're welcome."

"Why did you call her *hen*? That's rude." I appreciated the escape, but still.

He scrunched up his face. "Hen? I called her *Jen*. Her name is Jen."

Oh. I hadn't heard him correctly.

Maybe now I'd remember her name.

FLUTES OF CHAMPAGNE and cups of sparkling cider were being passed around as the year inched toward its final minutes. Couples moved to the dance floor or wandered off alone. At five minutes before midnight, Garrett and I were the only two at the table.

The temptation to do something I might regret—kissing him when the clock struck midnight—pounded in my chest. My fear wasn't gone. But my attraction—was it even just attraction now? My attraction was growing.

Acting more on panic, I hugged him. "I had fun tonight."

I tried not to notice the expectant look in his eyes.

"I did too. I'm glad you came."

Without another word, I jumped up and rushed out the side door. I didn't look back to see Garrett's reaction, but shock and disappointment were probably etched on his handsome face.

He deserved someone who could love him. Someone nice. Someone who could satisfy him.

Wiping tears, I dropped the tailgate on Eli's truck and sat

down. They could have their celebration, and I'd find him in a bit.

I'd promised myself I wouldn't think about my relationship with Garrett before the wedding, but everything made me think of Garrett. Why did I have to go and make things complicated?

As cheers erupted inside the building and a few fireworks exploded in the sky, a tall, chiseled figure strode toward me.

Garrett hooked a thumb over his shoulder. "It got loud, and everyone started kissing. I figured I'd join you out here." Instead of sitting down, he stopped in front of me. "If you want to talk, I'm willing to listen."

I just needed to tell him that I was afraid to discuss it before the wedding. He'd understand.

"I'm afraid..." Words evaporated, leaving me grasping for coherency. "I mean..."

"I know you're afraid." He stepped in between my legs and rested his hands on my hips. "Is that why you left?"

I shook my head, then nodded. "I'm afraid of what I want."

"What do you want?"

Staring at the buttons on his shirt, I blurted out an honest answer. "I want you to kiss me, and I want—"

His lips met mine with hunger and passion. Frozen, I urged myself to relax. I wanted this. So much.

He moaned, and that rumbly sound fueled me with a courage I didn't think possible. I felt desired. As I grasped his shirt, one of his hands found its way into my hair, and he tilted my head, giving him a better angle. I melted. My body reacted to his touch, to his kiss.

When he broke away, I leaned my head on his chest. His rapid heartbeat mimicked mine.

Close to my ear, he whispered, sending warmth dancing

down my neck. "I know why you're afraid. You can feel my heartbeat, can't you?"

"Yes." My answer escaped as a whisper.

"Does it feel disappointed?"

Still clutching his shirt, I held back sobs.

"Tessa, Skeeter was wrong. Or maybe he and I just want different things. Some men want notches on the bedpost and a string of conquests. Want to know what I want?"

I nodded against his chest.

"You." That one word was laced with more desire than I'd ever had directed at me.

"What if he was right?" Believing something for so long made it feel very true.

Garrett leaned back and cupped my chin. "He proved that he's not trustworthy." Before I could figure out what to say in response, he kissed my forehead, then pulled me to his chest. "This will be a busy week for you, and my timing probably wasn't great."

"Can we have the rest of this conversation after the wedding?"

"Just say when." He brushed a tear off my cheek. "Let me drive you home."

"Thanks." I slid off the tailgate and clasped Garrett's hand.

"You were about to say something else you wanted, but I sort of interrupted." He squeezed my hand.

"We'll talk in a week. If I start now, I'll be a blubbering mess, and I can't fall apart this week."

"That's fine. I can wait a week. And the image of you as a blubbering mess makes my chest ache, so don't do that." He opened the passenger door.

I hugged him. "Thank you for making this the best New Year's party ever. Sorry I ran out before the big toast."

His thumb brushed my cheek. "Happy New Year, Tessa. I hope this is the best one yet."

As Garrett pulled out of the venue, I texted Eli to let him know I had a ride home.

That was probably the plan all along.

The memory of Garrett's lips on mine would be a constant companion this week, and I wanted to believe him. Garrett was far more trustworthy than Skeeter. But what would it take for me to change my view of myself?

As we drove, he clasped my hand. With all the expected bustle and chaos, I needed his steadiness. And maybe a friendly soak in the hot tub.

CHAPTER 20

*A*s soon as I closed my shop on Wednesday, I drove out to the ranch and turned on the hot tub. The shop would be closed until after the wedding, and I wanted to enjoy a bit of quiet before the busyness of the next few days.

Garrett was working, and I didn't want to bother him, so I didn't mention my impromptu soak. But it wasn't quite the same being here alone.

I dropped my bag on the bed. This cabin wouldn't be a bad place to live. The place was furnished with basic pieces: a small table near the kitchenette, a couch and coffee table in the living room, and a bed and dresser in the bedroom. If I moved here, I'd either need to sell stuff or store it. As much as I wanted to live out here on the ranch, it would be so much harder to keep it friendly with Garrett. And any time a sprout of courage made me think dating Garrett wasn't such a big risk, fear showed up and trampled everything.

While idyllic in one way, the relationship I had with him wasn't fair to either of us. If I couldn't embrace the idea of a relationship, I'd have to pull away. But just like I'd let myself enjoy our atypical friendship for that week at the house, I gave myself permission to enjoy things as they were until after the wedding.

I changed into my swimsuit and pulled on the robe. As I turned to walk out to the porch, I spotted fuzzy slippers sitting beside the bedroom door. They were decorated to look like doughnuts with pink icing and sprinkles. On top of them was a note that read: *Saw these and thought of you.*

As I stared at the slippers, for some completely irrational reason, my brain pictured those cute little slippers as a metaphor for a romantic relationship with Garrett. They might fit perfectly. They would probably be warm and comfortable, but there was also the possibility that I'd slide my foot inside and my toes would meet a nasty scorpion. In these parts, it wasn't unusual to find a scorpion in your shoe.

Putting the slippers on included a risk, but by not putting them on, I'd never know which part was true.

After staring at them way too long, I padded outside in my bare feet and tossed my robe over the back of a chair, trying not to think about how much time and effort Garrett had put into my Christmas gift. In addition to the hot tub, there were several pieces of patio furniture and the screens. It was the perfect getaway.

Once I submerged in the warm water, I closed my eyes. The only thing left to do for the wedding was make the cakes, and I had all of tomorrow and part of Friday to make them. The cakes would be nothing short of fabulous because that was what my friends deserved.

My phone rang, and I answered the call on speaker. "Hi, Mom."

"Tessa, any news?"

"About?"

"Oh, you know… anything." She stayed quiet for almost a second. "Okay, fine. I'm asking about Garrett."

I hadn't mentioned to my mother that he'd given me a cabin and a hot tub because my parents would never buy the friendship story if they knew that.

"He's working at the ranch. So far, he really likes it."

"Good. But I wanted to know more about the two of you."

"We're still friends."

She sighed like a balloon being deflated. "I was afraid of that."

"How are you and Dad? Sorry I haven't called this week. It's been all wedding and doughnuts." I kept still so she wouldn't hear the water splashing.

"We're good. Your dad suggested that after Eli's wedding we go away on a second honeymoon. Our neighbor said they'd feed the cats and look after the dogs."

I looked at the phone as if that could in any way confirm that she'd actually said what I'd heard. "A second honeymoon?"

"Sounds romantic, doesn't it? Your dad isn't the gushy type, but sometimes he surprises me." I could hear the smile in her voice. "We've been seeing a counselor, and things are going well. There were lies I believed that were keeping me from a happier life. I'm dealing with those things now."

I needed my mom to get out of my head. This was not the time.

Boots sounded on the porch, and I turned and smiled up at Garrett.

"Hey, Tessa." His voice was deep and smooth.

"Hi, Garrett. I'll let you go, Tessa." Mom ended the call before I could say goodbye.

He glanced around the porch, then dropped into a chair. "Rough day?"

"Not too bad. But I'm not sure how much downtime I'll have until after the wedding is over. I almost texted you, but I figured you were out working."

179

"I was. When I spotted your car, I thought I'd pop by and say hi." He leaned forward and rested his elbows on his knees.

"Thank you for the slippers. They're super cute."

"Did they fit?"

Of course he would ask me that question.

"Not sure yet."

He stood and propped his hands on his head with his fingers laced together. "I should run, but if you *want* anything, call me. Or text me."

"I know." There was no question in my mind that no matter why or when, I could call Garrett and he'd show up to help me.

Who wouldn't want a friend like that?

* * *

LATE FRIDAY NIGHT after the pre-wedding festivities had ended, I eased into the warm water, the heat chasing away the cold. Staying at the cabin this weekend was a great choice. The rehearsal dinner and wedding were at the venue, and I had access to the hot tub.

"Knock, knock. Garrett's wine delivery service." He set two mugs down next to the hot tub, then shrugged off his coat and kicked off his flip-flops. "I didn't have any wine-glasses, so we're using mugs for our wine tonight."

I laughed at the matching cups. "You bought another friend mug."

"It just seems like the sort of mug there should be two of." He sighed as he stepped into the water. "This feels amazing. I'm glad I added the footpath from my front porch to your back porch. It's quite convenient."

"That *was* a good idea." I picked up a mug. "Thanks for the wine."

He sat next to me. "Think Delaney is going to get any sleep tonight?"

"Probably not. She and Eli will probably spend all night on the phone. It was fun watching them tonight at the rehearsal."

"All it takes is seeing them together for two minutes, and you know they love each other." He sipped his wine.

"I remember the first time they were in the same room. Eli barely said a word. He always acted that way when he met someone attractive. But somehow, in spite of all of his quiet and her rules, they figured out that they love each other. And I'm so excited about tomorrow because this makes them happy. Truly happy."

"And who doesn't want to be happy?"

"Exactly. Speaking of happy… how are you? How's life on the ranch? We haven't talked much this week." I worried the kiss at New Year's had changed something forever. For him. I knew it had for me. Inside, at least.

"I've been up with the sun every morning and working my butt off until after sundown every night, trying to learn about ranching. I've fallen asleep on my couch so many times this week. The only night I slept in my bed was the night I skipped sitting on the couch altogether and crawled under the covers as soon as I got home. That's why I hardly texted or called this week."

"Adjusting to a completely different schedule can be brutal." I knew that firsthand.

"How was your week?" He pulled one arm out of the water and stretched it out on the deck behind me.

"Good, but busy. I was closed Thursday and spent all day making the cakes for the wedding. Today, I've been helping Delaney stay calm. And thank you again for this amazing gift. Cami, Delaney, and I met here just before lunch and soaked in the hot tub while we discussed what things were left to be done. We were all more relaxed after that."

That gorgeous smile stretched across his face. "I'm glad you like it."

"Are you happy with your decision about changing careers?"

He nodded. "Very happy with my decision. I'm still kind of afraid I'll make a fool of myself a time or two. And I know it won't be easy. But the easiest things in life aren't always what will make you the happiest."

"I've never really thought about it that way."

"I've had to remind myself of that every time I've fallen off a horse, picked hay out of my hair, or been snagged by a barbed-wire fence. But nothing risked; nothing gained."

"I bet you're sore."

He nodded. "My muscles are adjusting."

I tapped his shoulder. "Move in front of me."

He shifted, and I set my mug on the edge, freeing up my hands. Slowly, I rubbed my thumbs into his shoulders, fighting through my hesitancy. Garrett and I had agreed we would finish the conversation after the wedding, and I knew he wouldn't bring it up tonight.

But I needed him to know I was trying, that I wanted this. Him.

After several minutes of silence as I massaged his sore body, he pulled my arms around him. "That felt amazing. Are you free every night?"

I rested my chin on his shoulder. "I'll check my calendar."

A shooting star darted across the sky.

I tapped his arm. "Did you see that?"

"Make a wish, Tessa." He moved behind me and pulled me into his lap.

I wished that in spite of my fear, I'd be brave enough to risk myself to gain… love. This wasn't about dating anymore.

I'd stupidly thought that not dating would mean never risking anything. Hogwash.

"Done. Did you make a wish?"

He pressed his cheek to mine, and I could feel his smile.

"I did, and maybe soon I'll tell you about it."

We sat snuggled in the hot tub as other stars streaked across the sky.

My fear wasn't gone, but I was learning to tame it and shut it up. And right now, I was content wrapped in Garrett's arms.

CHAPTER 21

*D*elaney stood in front of the mirror, pressing her hand to the bodice of her gown. "What do you think?"

I dabbed a tissue to my eyes, trying not to mess up my makeup. Hopefully, waterproof meant I wouldn't end the day with black streaks down my face. "You look incredible. Simply stunning. Eli won't know what to say."

"It won't be the first time." She laughed and blinked away tears. "Cami should be back here any second, so I'll make this quick. Don't end things with Garrett while I'm away on my honeymoon. *I beg you.* I won't be here to eat doughnuts with you, or to talk you into changing your mind. So, please—"

Cami stepped out of the other room with her arms spread wide. "How do I look?"

"Almost as good as Delaney." I hugged each of them. "I need to get my dress on so I'm not late for the ceremony."

Lilith poked her head in. "Do you ladies need anything?"

Delaney shook her head. "It's all great."

"And about to get better." Lilith glanced at the time. "I'll be back to check on y'all soon. Tessa, get dressed!"

I hurried into the other room and closed the door. As I slipped into the strapless cornflower-blue dress, I grinned at the idea that two of my favorite people in the whole world were embarking on a happily ever after. Their happily ever after had really started the day they'd met. It had just taken them both a little while to recognize that.

After freshening my lipstick and checking my hair, I joined Delaney and Cami. "I'm ready."

"Whoa! Look at you. Garrett is going to flip!" Cami had no trouble speaking her mind. "I already bet Delaney that Eli was going to try to get Mad Dog to hurry up the ceremony." With an arm around me and the other around Delaney, Cami lined us up in front of the massive mirror. "Look at us. Not only are we stunning, but look at how happy we are. So much has changed in such a short time. And if I keep talking, I'll cry, and then my makeup will look awful."

Delaney shifted to the middle and pulled us close. "I love y'all." The motorized cart pulled up outside, and she fanned her face. "It's time."

* * *

I HELD my breath to hold in my happy sobs as Eli slipped the ring on Delaney's finger.

His lip quivered a second. Then he smiled. "With this ring, I vow to love you, cherish you, and protect you forever and always."

Delaney promised Eli the same as she put a ring on his finger.

With tissues in each hand, her mom wiped away tears as her shoulders bounced.

By the time Mad Dog introduced Mr. and Mrs. Eli Gallagher to the world, there wasn't a dry eye in the place.

Eli and Delaney strolled down the aisle of the chapel, happier than I'd ever seen them.

Zach held out his arm to me, and we waited until the happy couple was out of the building before we started our exit.

"Someone is watching you." Zach wasn't all that subtle when he motioned toward Garrett.

I met Garrett's admiring gaze and felt my blood heat. My whole body was probably pink. Hopefully, Zach wouldn't say anything about that.

The wedding party clustered in the room beside the chapel while the guests made their way to the reception hall across the path.

Harper draped an arm around Cami. "Eli really took Mad Dog seriously when he said to kiss the bride. I think he's done it at least another dozen times since we've walked in here."

Delaney's cheeks flushed. "Sorry. We're just so—"

"Leave us alone." Eli pointed at Harper, then at Zach. "I have stories to tell about both of you. Be nice to me."

Zach shook his head. "That's not a threat. Haley knows all my stories."

Laughing we faced away from them, letting them enjoy a few minutes before they were hit with a wave of congratulations.

Lilith pushed open the door. "Delaney and Eli, y'all stay here another second. But the rest of you, come with me."

Cami laughed. "They'll be super disappointed about *being alone*."

Lilith escorted us into the chapel where Eli's and Delaney's families were waiting. "We'll get a few pictures out of the way, then grab the bride and groom."

After several minutes, Delaney and Eli joined us, and Lilith handed her a tube of lipstick.

The photographer continued shifting us around and snapping pictures.

While the bridesmaids were posing at the front, Garrett strolled into the chapel and stood in the back of the room. I'd seen magazine covers that didn't look as good.

He watched as we finished taking pictures.

The photographer looked at the screen on the back of her camera. "I think we're done. Thank you all for your patience."

Lilith clapped, trying to get everyone's attention. "The grand entrance is just going to be the bride and groom. The rest of you, please head over to the reception and get ready to cheer for our happy couple."

Garrett eased up beside me and held out his arm. I snuggled close to him as we hurried through the cold and into the reception hall.

"Would you like something to drink?" He shoved his hands in his pockets.

"Yes, but I'll go with you." I looped my arm around his and walked beside him as he made his way to the bar. "The ceremony was beautiful, wasn't it?"

"Very. I might've shed a few tears when Eli choked up during his vows, but that can be our secret." Garrett leaned in close, and his breath tickled my ear as he spoke. "You look fantastic, Tessa. Absolutely stunning."

"Thank you." I leaned against him. "You look very handsome in your suit. I've never seen you so dressed up."

"What can I get for you?" The bartender smiled.

Garrett looked down at me. "What would you like?"

"A glass of wine would be wonderful." I snuggled closer to him, appreciating his warmth.

"A glass of Moscato and a Shiner, please." Garrett shrugged off his suit coat. "I'm sorry. You must be cold in that dress."

"Just because we were outside for a minute. I'll warm up. You don't have to—"

"Please." He draped it around my shoulders. "For a few minutes."

"Thank you."

As the bartender handed over our drinks, the deejay called for everyone's attention.

"They're coming." I grabbed Garrett's hand and pulled him closer to the entrance.

The deejay raised his hand, and the crowd quieted. "Family and guests, please welcome the bride and groom, Delaney and Eli."

The doors opened, and Eli and Delaney strolled into the room hand in hand.

Garrett's hand tightened around mine. "Need a tissue?"

"Yes, but I didn't have anywhere to stash one." He let go of my hand and reached into his pocket. "I thought you might need these." He offered me a tissue from a small packet. "There are more in my pocket whenever you need them."

I dabbed at my eyes, then clasped his hand again. "You thought of everything."

"I was just thinking of you."

When Eli and Delaney made it to the middle of the dance floor, he kissed her, dipping her while everyone in the room cheered.

If I made it through the reception without my heart bursting open, it would be a miracle.

STANDING in the middle of the dance floor flanked by teenagers was not how I envisioned the bouquet toss. But I was thankful for Delaney's sisters. Otherwise, I'd be out here alone. The younger sister really wanted the bouquet, so I planned to step out of the way, but my plan fell apart when both sisters slapped at the bouquet like it was a volleyball. They were trying to keep it away from each other, but in the chaos, the flowers ended up in my hands.

After Delaney's sisters huffed off, I hugged my best friend.

"What magic did you use?" I couldn't figure out how I'd ended up with the bouquet.

"Love." She flashed a smile, then perched on a stool, ready for Eli to remove her garter.

"Single men, make your way to the dance floor." The deejay played an upbeat tune.

Ten or more men gathered. Garrett was out there, standing at the back of the crowd. It was probably good that he'd been shoved to the back because if he caught the garter, we'd have to take the traditional photos, and we'd hear about it forever.

I stepped out of the way but stayed close enough to see who would walk away with the prize.

Eli slipped off the blue, lacy garter and held it up. "You ready, guys?"

The group cheered.

With his back to the group, he tossed it over his head. Men dove for the lace, and when Garrett held his hand in the air, waving the garter, I smiled. That man never ceased to surprise me.

Delaney whispered to the deejay.

He pointed at Garrett. "Would the gentleman who caught the garter and the lady who caught the bouquet please come to the front."

Garrett sat down in the offered chair as I walked toward him. Grinning, he patted his knee, and I perched on his lap. The photographer snapped pictures of us and so did lots of other people, including my mother. Oh, I would for sure be hearing about this forever.

When I looked at Garrett, he smiled at me, and I could almost feel his lips on mine. The wedding wasn't over, but I was thinking about what I wanted and what I wanted to say.

How could I want something so much and still be afraid?

* * *

ELI KISSED Delaney before helping her stuff the wedding gown into the passenger seat of the truck.

"I love that they are leaving in his truck with her still in her wedding gown." I wiped tears off my cheeks with another tissue from Garrett's pack.

The truck pulled away, and I gave up wiping tears. Eli and Delaney were married.

As the crowd headed back inside, Garrett put his arm around me. "I need to help Dad with a few things, but when I'm done, would you like to talk in the hot tub?"

It would be so easy to say yes to the hot tub. But the easiest wasn't always the best. Garrett was right about that.

"Not tonight." I hugged him. "We'll talk tomorrow."

Though he tried to hide it, his disappointment was obvious, but I couldn't focus on that. I'd spent a lot of time pushing him away. Emotionally, at least. I wasn't great at pushing him away otherwise.

I needed to figure out what to say because even though I loved him, I wasn't ready if he asked for more.

* * *

WEARING exercise leggings and a baggy sweatshirt, I peeked out to make sure Garrett's truck wasn't parked out front.

Since the coast was clear, I climbed into my car and drove

to town. I needed a few ingredients that I didn't typically keep on hand. After buying what I needed, I hurried to the doughnut shop. Right now, I wanted to make doughnuts. More than that, I wanted to eat doughnuts.

I kept the lights off in front, made sure the blinds were closed, and set to work in the kitchen.

CHAPTER 22

GARRETT

*T*he night before the wedding and at the ceremony, the signals I was getting from Tessa had rippled excitement through me. When she looked at me, there was desire in her gaze, but then she hadn't wanted to talk tonight. As I changed out of my suit and thought about every look and word we'd exchanged, I wondered if I'd misread her.

Chores weren't enough of a distraction. Tonight, they were tiresome because they kept me away from her.

An hour later, I was still wondering and replaying every smile, every brush of her skin on mine.

I hadn't kept my feelings a secret. She knew how I felt, and I had to let her make the choice to reciprocate those feelings. I couldn't make her love me.

I'd be on edge until she decided she wanted to talk.

Slogging through the chores that needed to be done, I kept thinking back to the look Tessa gave me when she'd perched in my lap. Remembering that look, I wanted to believe that she loved me. I hoped…

It was after ten when I parked in front of my cabin, and I

sat in my truck staring at the empty parking space in front of hers. Her car was gone.

My concern changed to mild panic, and I sent her a text. *Tessa, please call me.*

Earlier when she'd said we'd talk tomorrow, I lost a little hope that she'd get past her fear. Now that her car was gone, so was the rest of my hope.

I sat on the couch with my front door open, listening for her car to return.

Hours later, I woke up still sitting on my couch. I ran outside as I checked my phone. Her car still wasn't here, and she hadn't texted or called. It was three in the morning, and I wouldn't be able to sleep until I knew she was safe.

Maybe she'd gone back to her apartment. If her car was there, I'd have a different problem to face, but at least I'd know where she was.

Fishing keys out of my pocket, I ran to my truck. It was tomorrow already, and when I found Tessa, I'd say everything I hadn't said. How could I convince her that I wasn't like Skeeter? I wouldn't take her love for granted, cheat on her, or wound her intentionally. I called her again before starting the engine, but it went straight to voice mail.

Kicking up dust, I tore out of the ranch and headed toward town. The ten-minute drive had never seemed so long.

I turned into her complex and circled the lot at a crawl, hoping to spot her car. I gave up after three loops because someone was bound to call in a suspicious vehicle.

When I made the obligatory stop before turning on to the main road, I noticed her car parked in front of the doughnut shop. She wasn't supposed to open tomorrow. Why was she there making doughnuts?

Immediately my thoughts jumped to our conversation on

the rooftop patio. She'd made doughnuts during the night while she was closed after Skeeter dumped her.

Preparing myself to find her in tears and eating way too many doughnuts, I pulled into the lot and parked next to her car.

The lights didn't seem to be on, but the blinds were closed. I peeked through the space created by the bent end of one slat. Lights were on in the kitchen. She had to be here. But why?

Pounding on the door, I prepared myself for a conversation I didn't want to have. "Open up, Tessa. It's me."

Peering through the tiny gap, I watched as she ran toward the door. She stopped in the middle of the room when her doughnut slipper came off.

Smiling, she pulled the door open, and her eyes widened. "Garrett! Why aren't you asleep?"

Her leggings were covered in flour, her sleeves pulled up to her elbows, and she'd skipped the apron altogether. There was chocolate smeared on her face and a half-eaten doughnut in her hand.

"What are you doing here in the middle of the night?" She backed up, giving me room to walk in.

"Freaking out. I was worried because you didn't answer your phone."

She glanced at her purse on the counter. "Sorry. It's been off for hours. My mom called, and I didn't want to talk to her tonight, so I turned off my phone. I'm sorry."

"What's wrong, Tessa?" I moved closer, hoping she wouldn't back away.

She tucked a strand of hair back into her messy bun. "I just look horrible because I haven't slept." Biting her lip, she kicked up one foot. "But my slippers fit perfectly. They are really comfortable."

She didn't look horrible. She looked adorable, incredible, and beautiful. But before I told her that, I needed to figure out why she was making doughnuts in the middle of the night.

"Why are you here?"

Smiling, she walked to the counter and broke pieces off a doughnut. "Rather than explain why, I'll just show you." She popped one piece in her mouth, then stood in front of me. "Open up."

I caught her around the wrist. "Please tell me what's wrong. You're eating doughnuts."

Her brown eyes twinkled with what looked like—and what I hoped was—a flirty tease.

"Of course I'm eating doughnuts. How else would I know if the new flavors taste good?"

"New flavors?" We were both speaking English, but I was lost in our conversation.

After licking her lips, she touched my cheek. "Open your mouth."

I did as requested, and once again, Tessa fed me. Having her feed me when I wasn't in pain and helpless was, by far, a better experience. Cinnamon and sugar filled my senses. "This tastes like my grandma's cookies."

Her smile widened, and she ran back to the counter. "Now try this one." Her fingers brushed my lips as she fed me the other piece. "What do you think?"

"I think it tastes like a chocolate chip cookie and a doughnut all mixed into one. It's delicious."

"Good." She squared her shoulders. "Because I made them for you. I have so many things I want to say, but because I haven't slept, I can't remember most of them. But I remember two things." She held up two fingers. "Wait three." Another finger joined the others. "Before Thanksgiving, I kept thinking that my two best friends were getting married, but you changed that. Now when I think about Eli and Delaney, I think that two *of* my best friends got married. You added an of to my life." Stepping closer, she rested a hand on my chest. "You've become one of my best friends."

The word "friends" was not what I was hoping to hear. I steeled my reaction and smiled because that was how I was supposed to react when someone said I was their best friend.

And she wasn't wrong. We were friends, but I wanted so much more.

"You know that I was afraid of disappointing you, but after the wedding when I told you we'd talk tomorrow, the hurt and disappointment on your face made me realize something else. Hurting you was never my intention."

All this talk of hurting me had me nauseous. I met her gaze, bracing for words I hoped would never come. "Tessa, you don't need to worry about disappointing me."

Her lips pinched together as she rested her other hand on my chest, and her gaze dropped to my shirt.

If she couldn't even look at me, this wasn't going to be good.

"And the second thing, I mean the third…" Tears glistened in her eyes as she stared at my buttons.

I was about to become a sympathy crier. "Tessa, please tell me."

"I love you."

Her words landed like a toddler on a trampoline, and somewhere deep inside, I felt the same giddy joy as that kid. I'd been waiting for her to say I had a chance or that she'd go out with me, but she'd skipped right past all that. I was stunned speechless.

She licked her lips and looked up at me. "I know it's customary for me to let you say that first, but I needed to say that. If you don't feel that way, please tell me right now while I have plenty of doughnuts to eat." Her gaze stayed fixed on mine as she waited for me to respond. "I'm not ready to sleep with you. Yet. But—"

Words were insufficient right now. I caught her lips with mine and backed her toward the counter.

When she couldn't back up anymore, she broke the kiss. "You have no idea how many times I've thought about doing this."

"Believe me. I have a pretty good idea." I kissed her again, blindly making sure a spot on the counter was clear before lifting her onto it.

She circled her arms around my neck and kissed me more fervently.

After several minutes, I pulled back and brushed my thumb across her lips. "I've thought about kissing you multiple times a day, sometimes multiple times an hour, since not kissing you in the hot tub. And after New Year's, I thought about it twice as often."

"I can't wait to kiss you in the hot tub." She tugged me back to her and wrapped her legs around my waist. "And in the cabin." She pressed a kiss to my stubble. "And by the barn." Her lips brushed mine. "And on the hilltop with the amazing view."

"There is so much of the ranch you haven't seen. So much of it I want to show you." I crushed her to my chest and held her, helped by the fact that her legs were wrapped around me.

"I remembered one other thing I needed to say. Later, I'm sure I'll remember the other stuff." She rested her forehead against mine.

"What's the other thing?"

"I want to move into the cabin if it's really okay."

"Yes. It's okay. More than okay." All my dreams were coming true in this little doughnut shop in the middle of the night. Well, not all of them, but there was a perfect time for everything.

"Good. Because I want to be able to see you at the end of every day, laugh with you over dinner in the dining hall, and enjoy a more-than-friendly soak in the hot tub with you when you have time."

"I love you, Tessa. I hope my actions have been clear about that. And I'm not asking for more right now. When I carry you to my bed, there will be a ring on your finger, and I don't mean an engagement ring."

She hugged me, her grin wide and tears glistening in her eyes. "I fell in love with you when we were only friends. Wait! Did you plan it that way?"

"We can talk about that tomorrow." I didn't want to mess up a good thing.

Her head wagged back and forth. "No. Seriously. Did you?"

"I knew you were afraid of dating and getting hurt. My hope was that you'd see that you could trust me. Love is a lot like friendship. It's about spending time together, laughing together, and crying together. So, yeah, I was hoping to sneak into your heart through the friend zone."

She kissed the scar just under my eye. "You knew exactly what I needed. You showed me that you're..." She crinkled her nose, then teared up. "You're perfect for me."

"I want to be, Tessa."

She teased her fingers through my hair. "Isn't it funny that we're saying we love each other in the same place where you asked me out the very first time?"

Her smile made it seem like she remembered that day fondly. My take on it was a bit different.

"Quite funny. Especially considering that you turned me down." I kissed her again before setting her on her feet. "Let's get you home and to bed."

"I'm going to have a sugar crash very soon. I haven't eaten anything but doughnuts since the wedding, and I haven't slept a wink."

"What do I need to do to get us out of here? I'll come back later and help you clean."

"Gosh. I sure made a mess. I'm usually not this messy in the kitchen." She ran around behind the counter. "Put all those doughnuts in here." She laid out flat boxes. "I forgot to tell you what they're called. These are my after-school flavors. After-school snickerdoodle and after-school chocolate chip."

She'd definitely be an after-school cookies kind of mom, but that was a conversation for another day.

I started packing doughnuts into boxes. In one of them, I mixed the flavors and labeled that one with my name. That particular box was headed to my cabin. The rest could go to the dining hall.

"I'm ready. Everything perishable is put away." She covered a yawn.

I lifted the stack of boxes. "We'll come back for your car."

"Good idea." She pushed open the door, then ran back to the counter for her purse. "I'm glad you love me."

I'd spend the next hundred years thinking the same thing.

* * *

BEFORE WE MADE it even halfway back to the ranch, Tessa was asleep. Her fingers were laced with mine, and her lips were curved into a smile.

Once we passed through the gate, I drove to the main house at a snail's pace, relishing every moment. After gently sliding my hand out of hers, I ran the doughnuts into the dining hall before driving to the cabins.

As I slid out of the truck, I texted Ava. *Tessa created two new flavors. Enjoy. I might be late to breakfast.*

Ava replied right away. *I'll keep breakfast tacos warm for you. Everything okay?*

She loves me.

I already knew that. Ava followed her text with a laughing emoji and a heart.

When I opened the passenger-side door, Tessa's eyes fluttered open. "Sorry. I didn't mean to fall asleep."

Her dark hair draped across her face when she turned to look at me.

I was the luckiest man alive. "You are beautiful. I know I wasn't allowed to say that before, but I hope it's okay now."

Smiling, she bobbed her head. "More than okay. I like it when you call me beautiful... and fantastic... and stunning."

"Good. Let's get you into bed, my beautiful, fantastic, and stunning friend."

She unbuckled her seat belt and climbed out of the truck. "I like being your friend. But I think I'm really going to like being your girlfriend."

"I'll make sure you do." I swept her off her feet and carried her inside. After laying her in the bed and pulling off her slippers, I kissed her on the forehead. "Sleep. I'll be back later."

Her brow furrowed. "I messed up your sleep, and now you have to work. I'm sorry. I didn't think about that when I turned off my phone."

"No apologies. I'll be back later. And after I sleep, we'll soak in the hot tub."

"And kiss?"

"Yes, ma'am." I planned to do a lot of kissing in the hot tub.

CHAPTER 23

*A*fter sleeping for seven glorious hours, I rolled out of bed. It had been the best sleep I'd had in months... probably because I wasn't lying to myself anymore. I took a quick shower, then threw on jeans and a sweater. I had a shop to clean, but the first order of business was to find Garrett.

My Garrett.

I walked into the living room and smiled. He was stretched out on my couch with his feet propped up on one end. The couch wasn't big enough to fit his tall frame.

On the coffee table, was a box of doughnuts, and several were missing.

I knelt beside the couch and admired the man who'd shown me that love and friendship had lots in common. My fingers itched to trace the small scar below his right eye, a forever reminder of what had happened at Thanksgiving and the week we'd spent together.

With a book in one hand and a doughnut in the other, I sat with my back to the couch and read and ate. I wanted to be here when he woke up.

A half hour later, the couch creaked before warm fingers brushed hair out of the way, and Garrett dropped kisses on my neck.

"Mmm. Good morning, cowboy."

Chuckling he sat up. "Are you going to miss *the spy?*"

I nestled into his lap and kissed his scar. "You'll always be my *cowboy spy*. Lots of integrity and a little bit of mystery." I combed my fingers through his brown wavy hair. "Think we can keep the move quiet until after Delaney and Eli get back?"

He scrunched up his face. "Maybe. In this town, all it takes is one person to see you carrying a box out of your apartment, and word will spread like glaze on a hot doughnut."

"We should at least try. I'm going to get some food and then go clean. After that, I'm going to get boxes and start packing. You can sleep more."

"I'm good. When dad found out that I hadn't slept much, he sent me home. So I slept on your couch." His smile made the implication abundantly clear.

I was home for him, which was perfect because I felt the same way.

Garrett checked the time. "If we go now, we'll make it over to the dining hall in time for lunch."

"Good because I'm starving." I put on my shoes while he pulled on his boots. "Where's your hat?"

"In the truck." He laced his fingers with mine as we walked out the door. "When is your lease up?"

"End of the month. I was supposed to let them know at the end of December if I wasn't going to renew, and I'd told them I probably wouldn't but that I'd let them know for sure after this weekend."

"You liked me." Those blue eyes twinkled with the mischief of a little boy as he opened the truck door.

"A lot." After climbing in, I grabbed his shirt before he stepped away. "You clearly get me, so you probably already figured this out, but…" I could say anything to Garrett, and now that my heart was unmistakably on the butchering slab, I was about to hand Garrett the cleaver. "If you ask me to marry you, I'm going to say yes. And when I'm married to you, I'll sleep with you. I'll want to. But I don't want a long engagement. The shorter the better."

Grinning, he leaned in and gave me a quick peck. "I'll remember that." He cupped my cheek. "I love you, and my heart is yours. To you, I will always be faithful."

I leaned into his hand. "When you didn't kiss me that night, you showed me you were safe. And strong."

"I'm glad you like my kind of muscles."

"And when you did kiss me at New Year's, it was impossible to ignore what I felt for you."

Smiling, he patted my leg before closing the door.

I watched him run around to the driver's side.

He climbed in, then leaned over and kissed me. "I'm glad you love me."

Clutching his hand, I watched out the window as he drove to the main house. "You kept showing up. I need steady. Scratch that. I *want* someone steady."

"Steady, huh? Some people call it stubborn." He winked as he parked the truck.

When we walked into the dining hall hand in hand, everyone clapped. I inched up and kissed Garrett, which garnered some cheers and whistles. What hadn't been obvious to me had been obvious to everyone here, and I loved that for some weird reason.

Parker laughed. "Friends, huh? I need a friend like that."

Garrett grinned as we sat down. "Normally, I'd give getting beaten up zero stars, but well… totally worth it." He bumped my shoulder. "She didn't even run me over."

* * *

Just like he promised, Garrett helped me clean the shop, and then we started packing up my apartment. And after we'd cleaned and packed for several hours, the hot tub felt magical.

He eased into the water after me, and I didn't hesitate to snuggle into his lap. "Why did you ask me out that day?"

"Does it matter?" He nuzzled my neck.

"I want to know."

"I heard you defending Eli to the two women in the doughnut shop. You know, the one who wanted you to introduce her at New Year's."

I remembered. "They were the typical mean girls in high school. And some people don't change. I still can't believe she asked me if I'd introduce her to you at the New Year's Eve party."

"But you weren't rude to them. In the doughnut shop, you just stuck up for Eli and Delaney. At the party, it was cute that you didn't want to introduce me. I liked that."

"So you asked me out because of how I treat people?"

"Part of the reason. Then you showed your true colors." His arms tightened around me. "That night on the side of the road, I was scared. I don't think I've ever said that. More than one car drove past me that night, and the later it got, the more despair I felt. I was in so much pain, and it was cold. I'd never been more miserable. But then you showed up."

I blinked away tears.

"You could've decided that it was too scary to help a stranger in the dark alone, but you did more than just help me into the car and take me to the hospital. You cared. And that meant so much to me." He kissed my head. "Also, you're extremely attractive."

"I'm glad you think so, and I'm glad you moved here." I

tilted my head back to look at him. "I really missed eating doughnuts."

A chuckle rumbled in his chest as his lips met mine. Without breaking away, I turned and wrapped my arms around him, sitting sideways in his lap. With one arm holding me close and another tangled in my hair, he tilted my head, finding the perfect angle.

For several minutes, he kissed me like a man who'd been craving it for months.

This hot tub was now my favorite place in the whole world. Really, anywhere with Garrett was my favorite place.

"Last night, I told you I couldn't remember all the things I wanted to say. I'm not even sure I can remember them all now. Thoughts were bouncing around in my head as I made doughnuts. But there are a few things I want you to know. I'd convinced myself that not dating was the way to avoid the risk of being humiliated again. But spending a week with you was like gasoline on my spark of attraction. And at first, that's all it was. You're attractive. And well built. Rather hot, actually. I was attracted to you."

Garrett nuzzled my neck. "Keep talking. I'm listening."

"But the more time I spent with you, the more those feelings changed into something deeper, and that outweighed my fear. I felt loved, and when I admitted to myself that I loved you..." I chewed my bottom lip, trying to find the right words. "I guess love chased out my fear."

His lips captured mine, and his kiss felt like a promise of forever. When he broke away, he closed his eyes and sighed. "I think I'm going to like having you closer."

"I'm going to love it." I dropped kisses on his shoulder and along his shoulder blade. "The reason I didn't talk to you in the hot tub after the wedding was because I wanted to show you how much you meant to me, like you showed me over and over again. But I wasn't sure how to do that until the very end of the wedding. Maybe it was the groom's cake that sparked the idea. And then I needed time to create the flavors."

"Having Eli's cake shaped like a doughnut was awesome."

"Those two fell in love over doughnuts, so it was fitting. Have you texted Eli?"

"No. The man is on his *honeymoon*."

"Good. I'll tell them about us when they get back. I should probably call my mom. I did text her, but I just said I was busy enjoying my day off and that I'd talk to her later. They are on a second honeymoon. I don't want to bother them. She's going to be excited though. They really like you." I had no doubt my parents would be excited about my decision. "Oh, and Mom sent me the picture she took of me sitting in your lap."

"She sent it to me too. It's a good picture." He poked me in the side. "I like the way you're looking at me in that picture."

"I promised myself I wouldn't think about us until after the wedding, but I thought about you all the time. Then all those guys dove for the garter, but you so coolly raised your hand holding it. I don't know how you did it, but it made me think you'd fight for me. That's a silly thing to assume from a garter toss, I guess." I traced his jawline with the tip of my finger. "It's possible I was thinking about our kiss when I was in your lap."

"That explains a lot. And I'm hoping I didn't accidentally break anyone's finger or anything, but I was pretty set on walking away with that lacy little thing." He brushed his lips on my ear. "I was also pretty set on keeping my promise to you… to expend all my energy to win your heart."

"I figured out what you meant later that same day when I shared my fears with Delaney. She said you'd show me if you wanted more than friendship. Then you gave me this." I dragged my hand through the water, stirring up the bubbles.

"I'm looking forward to all the Christmas mornings we'll spend together and all the new years we'll ring in with a kiss. And maybe more than a kiss."

The gravel in his voice made me hope he wouldn't wait too long to propose. I wanted him. All of him.

"I know I've asked you this before, but why did you help me?" He danced his lips on my neck, trailing kisses on my skin.

"I was afraid, but fear shouldn't be an excuse to leave another person in pain."

He met my gaze. "Now I love you more. But I didn't mean on the side of the road. I was talking about after that. Why risk it? You could've just left me at the hospital."

"You needed my help."

He waited, clearly not satisfied with my answer.

"Your dad is well-known for his integrity and generosity, so when I found out you were his son, it didn't seem like that much of a risk."

"You had no way of knowing that I wasn't a horrible person." He brushed a wet hair off my face.

"I knew. Before I knew who you were, I knew. Getting you into the car caused you so much pain, and yet, you focused on wiping away my tears. Horrible people don't do that." I touched his cheek. "And Eli offered to set me up with you, and he'd never done that before. With anyone."

"Remind me to thank him."

"And you kept holding my hand. It felt good."

Garrett kissed me. Over and over again.

I was going to love dating this tall, chiseled brick.

CHAPTER 24

I scanned my apartment. There were a few items of furniture that needed to go into storage and a few that needed to be sold, but everything else was either at the cabin or in the bed of Garrett's truck.

He eased up behind me and circled his arms around me. "Everything that's left goes to the storage unit?"

"Mostly. I'm selling the couch. What about the table and chairs?" I didn't want to store something I wouldn't want when I emptied stuff from storage.

"Do you like it?"

"It's okay, but it's not something I'd put in my dream home. If that makes sense."

"Sell it."

"Let me take some pictures. I'm not posting anything until Delaney gets back. Because she'll see the posts, and then my surprise will be ruined."

Garrett squinted and cocked his head. "What are you planning, Tessa?"

I flashed what I hoped was an innocent-looking smile. "A surprise."

"Details." One eyebrow lifted. The man had no clue how hot he was.

"I'm going to leave a post-it note on the door that says MOVED-Call Me. That's it. Nothing bad."

He laughed. "I hope I'm around when Delaney and Eli find you."

"They are supposed to be back tonight. I don't figure they'll show up at my apartment until tomorrow." I locked the door and followed him to the truck.

"How did today go at the shop?"

"Good." I waited until he slid behind the wheel to share my other surprise. "I interviewed someone today."

He snapped his head to face me. "You did what?"

"I can't work every single day like I used to. Even if I just train someone to run the store and only have to show up to make doughnuts, that's better than what I've been doing. It's not healthy."

He grabbed my hand. "How'd it go?"

"She starts Tuesday. Now I just need to find someone who likes to make doughnuts. Oh, I also decided that I'm going to start closing on Mondays. The weekends are busy, and being closed that day just makes sense." I'd looked at the books and knew that hiring two people and closing one day a week wasn't going to put me in the red.

Squeezing my hand, he backed out of the parking spot. "You amaze me, Tessa. I'll do my best not to let work—"

"Stop. I know you are learning about the ranch and that it takes time. I also see the role model you have. It may have taken your dad more than a year to take Lilith on an exotic honeymoon, but he made it work. And the best part, it's not just you running the ranch. One day, when Clint decides to retire, you'll find another foreman who will run things with the same skill." I rubbed his arm. "You're a rancher. Hours may vary. I know that, and I'm totally fine with that."

He pulled my fingers to his lips. "Thank you. I needed to hear that."

"I love you. I love that you're Mr. Henry now, but you'll always be my Mr. Right."

"You're the *best*."

* * *

ELI PULLED open the door to the shop, and Delaney ran up to the counter.

She held up the note in front of my face. "Does this mean what I think it means?"

"I'm surprised you found that already." I pulled two doughnuts out of the case, one of each of the newest additions. "Want to try my new flavors?"

Eli leaned over Delaney's shoulder. "Yes. What kind are they?"

"Taste them."

She shook her head. "First I want to know the answer." She glanced at the few people sitting at tables, then grabbed my left hand. "I had to check."

I rolled my eyes. Her reaction made my news seem anticlimactic.

"Leaning forward, I whispered, "I moved to the ranch… into *my own* cabin."

Her eyes narrowed. "You didn't break things off with Garrett?"

"Of course she didn't." Eli licked his fingers. "Didn't you see the way she looked at him when they posed for pictures at the reception? I like both of them, but the cinnamon one is my favorite."

Delaney's jaw dropped open. "You ate both of them? Did you leave me even a bite?"

As he pulled out his wallet, Eli flashed his get-out-of-trouble smile, which usually worked on everyone except his mom. "Tessa, could I get two doughnuts? The new flavors."

"Coming right up." I set them on the counter. "Do y'all want coffee?"

Delaney nodded. "I want a cup, but none for him."

"I have to figure out how to sleep today so I can work tonight."

"Go soak in the hot tub. It's very relaxing." I handed Delaney a to-go cup. "Then you'll be able to sleep."

She pressed a kiss to Eli's cheek. "Maybe I should open late and come join you."

"No hanky-panky in my hot tub. Get your own if you want to do that." I laughed as Eli spun around and walked right out the door.

"The two of you crack me up. Y'all are more like siblings than cousins." Delaney took a bite of a doughnut and gasped. "This is amazing."

"I'm glad you like it. Garrett inspired the new flavors."

"Interesting. Since you didn't argue with Eli, I'm guessing he's right. And I want to hear all about it. You free tonight?"

"I'd love to get together. Text me." I ran around the counter and hugged her. "And I want to hear about *your* week. But only parts of it."

She grabbed the other doughnut. "Noted. I'm off to the store… to order myself a few new things."

I covered my ears. "Don't want to hear it."

Laughing, Delaney waved over her shoulder as she strolled out. "I like the chocolate chip flavor best."

* * *

I WATCHED as Delaney settled herself in the hot tub. "It's perfect, isn't it? I'm in love."

"With him or with the hot tub?" Delaney splashed me.

"Yes."

She waved her hands. "Start at the beginning. Eli and I left the reception, and…"

"And Garrett asked if I wanted to talk in the hot tub after he finished up with ranch chores. I told him no because I wanted time to think."

"Tessa! That poor man."

"Yeah. And then I snuck away to the shop and made doughnuts all night. With my phone off. I knew the gist of what I wanted to say to him, but I wanted it to be more than words. I wanted to show him like he'd shown me."

Her eyes widened.

"Garrett pounded on the door at three in the morning. I felt bad that I'd worried him, but his coming after me in the middle of the night was just another confirmation that he's what I want." I smiled as a figure walked around the privacy screen.

"Knock, knock. Garrett's wine delivery service." He tipped his hat. "I'm not going to crash your party, but I thought y'all might be thirsty."

"See what I mean. He's perfect."

Garrett winked as he handed me a mug. "Holler if you need anything else. I can't promise I'll be awake more than five minutes after sitting down, but you can try." He blew me a kiss before strolling away, whistling as he went.

"I'm so happy for you." Delaney sipped her wine. "And this is the part where I get to say I told you so. Garrett completely swept you off your feet."

"Yep. And it all started with dragging him to my car. Not exactly the typical *once upon a time*."

CHAPTER 25

*A*fter a month of having help, I wondered how I had ever run the shop alone.

I parked outside the main house at the ranch and carried bags of doughnuts into the dining hall. The ranch hands had agreed to taste test for me. And I knew they'd be honest about it.

After unloading the bags, I opened the boxes in the middle of the table. "All right, guys. Thank you so much for doing this. Since Layla is helping me run the counter, I've had time to train my new hire. She's kind of a natural when it comes to making doughnuts, but this is the real test. She made all the doughnuts in two of these boxes, And I made all the doughnuts in the other two. Taste test away."

The ranch hands and Mason all grabbed doughnuts.

"Make sure you know which is which." I folded my arms, waiting rather impatiently for the verdict.

Still chewing, Archer nodded. "They're good."

"Good?" I needed more than that.

"They taste the same." He picked up another one. "And

whoever it is that makes doughnuts as good as you, I want to meet her."

"That can be arranged." I could give Cami another matchmaking project. "She's new in town, so I'm sure she'd love to meet new people."

Parker nudged Archer. "Hear that? She'd *love* to meet you."

"Hey, tagalong, leave Archer alone." I tossed a wadded-up napkin at Parker. "Be nice."

He feigned shock. "I'm always nice. Ask Mason. Right?"

With a doughnut in each hand and one in his mouth, the kid grinned and pointed at one of Lettie's boxes. "I like those better. Who made those?"

Now I was satisfied. If I went on vacation, my customers would still get the doughnuts they loved.

Garrett hung his hat on the hook as he walked into the dining room. "Verdict?"

I scanned the group. "Everyone agree?"

Dag gave a thumbs-up. "They're all great. I agree with Archer that they taste the same."

One at a time, they all said the same thing... except Mason. "Those are better... because I found a sprinkle in that box. And I like sprinkles."

"I cannot argue with that logic." Garrett tousled the kid's hair. "Sounds like success to me."

"Me too." I picked up a doughnut out of Lettie's box. "These are great!"

"Of course they are." Garrett picked up a doughnut and took a bite. "You made this one, I think. Am I right?"

I shook my head, then kissed his cheek. "And I'm thrilled you can't tell."

"Whew. Want to take a drive with me?"

"Lead the way, cowboy." I motioned to the boxes. "Enjoy, but don't let Mason have too many more. He might explode."

Parker laughed. "I'm pretty sure he's had more than two. Isn't that what your dad said was the limit?"

"Three is close to two. I just lost count." Mason licked his fingers. "They're really good."

Garrett laced his fingers with mine, and it dawned on me that I hadn't seen him shove his hands in his pockets once since that night at my shop.

"You used to have your hands in your pockets when you were around me. Now you don't."

"I don't now because I'm usually holding your hand. I did then because I wanted to hold your hand."

I kissed him before buckling my seat belt. "Mom called. She wants us to come for dinner."

"Tonight?"

"Tomorrow. Are you free? If you don't want to go, I understand. I'll try to schedule it for a different day, or maybe just go by myself."

He squeezed my hand. "Tomorrow night is fine. I'll let Dad and Clint know."

We turned out of the ranch and drove toward the goat farm, but he continued past Joji's gate. A half mile past her place, he turned left and punched a code into a small box.

A large gate swung open, and Garrett shot me a side glance as he pulled through onto what looked like a new gravel road. "It'll be paved, but we can get up there in the truck now."

"The hilltop?"

"After talking to Dad and getting feedback on cost and possibilities, I decided that up there was the perfect place to build."

He didn't add "our home" to the end of his sentence, but I heard it just the same.

As soon as he stopped rolling, I jumped out. "I love it. It reminds me of the rooftop."

He slipped his arms around me. "It does. But it'll take a while to build a house, so I'm trying to be patient. It's not easy though."

"You not patient? Whatever." I rested my head against his chest. "This will be worth the wait."

* * *

THE SHOP WAS extra busy for a Tuesday morning. Lilith, Joji, and Ava had come in for an early sweet snack. Cami and Delaney sat at the table visiting with them even though Delaney's store was supposed to open in twenty minutes.

When I had a free minute, I stopped at their table. "Can I get y'all anything else?"

"We're good. Just enjoying the yummy doughnuts and conversation." Joji smiled.

"Holler if you do. I'm going to make a fresh pot of coffee."

It was a luxury to have someone manning the counter, and Layla did a great job interacting with customers.

The door opened, and I turned to offer a welcome. "Welcome to Sweets—Nico, hi!"

He waved, but his gaze was fixed on Layla. And Layla—who was never shy—flushed pink and looked down at the counter.

"Good morning." He leaned down to catch her eye. "How are you today?"

"Really good. Thank you." Her smile brightened as her gaze met his. "What can I get you?"

Clearly there was a story there, and once I had a chance to talk to Layla alone, I'd gather information. I was surprised they even knew each other.

When the door opened again, I gave up watching Nico and Layla and turned to see who'd walked in. "Garrett, this is a nice surprise."

"I had a craving... for this." He cupped my cheek and kissed me like he'd done a month ago in the middle of the night.

Grinning, I shot a glance at the table I knew was watching. "Wow."

His fingers threaded with mine. "I know you've heard jokes about being the *best* girl, but of all the women in the world, you are most definitely the *best* one for me." Still holding my hand, he dropped to one knee, and the hum of conversation halted as everyone watched in hushed silence. "Tessa Best, will you do me the honor of becoming Mrs. Henry? I could search the world over, and I'd never find anyone more *right* for me. I want to spend my life with you, to laugh with you, and even cry with you. Will you marry me?"

"Yes." I launched toward him, nearly knocking the ring out of his hand.

But skilled as he was, he managed to hang onto it and still catch me.

Cheers broke out all over the room. I was too busy kissing Garrett to see the smiles at one table, but I knew those ladies were all happy for me and in on this surprise.

With me perched on his knee, he slid the ring on my finger. "If you aren't busy right now, I'd like to go to the courthouse."

"Let me grab my purse." I started to get up, then turned and kissed him again. "I said yes already, didn't I?"

"You did, and everyone here heard you."

Laughter echoed off the walls.

Layla handed me my purse. "I've got this place covered. Have fun."

Garrett smiled all the way to his truck. "I'm hoping we can convince a judge to waive the three-day wait. Because dinner with your parents has been moved to the dining hall, and I booked the house in San Antonio for the next five nights."

"The house?"

"Yep. I've been waiting until you didn't have to close the shop to have a getaway. But if we can't get a waiver, the guy handling reservations said he'd make an exception and let me shift the dates." Garrett parked in front of the courthouse.

There were benefits to living in a small town. It didn't take us long to drive here, the judge knew the Henry family, and we walked out of the courthouse with a marriage license and a waiver.

By the time we pulled away from the courthouse, everyone in the county had probably heard that Garrett and I were engaged.

CHAPTER 26

*G*arrett drove up to our hilltop. "When we were up here yesterday, it was very hard not to propose right then." He dropped the tailgate, then pulled a quilt out of his back seat.

I climbed up and sat down beside him once he had everything arranged.

"I only waited this long to propose because I didn't want you to have to close the shop again so soon after the holidays and the wedding. And the house in San Antonio was booked solid." He opened the cooler. "I brought food if you're hungry."

"I love that we're going back to the house." I patted my leg. "Lie down."

He rested his head in my lap. "I didn't plan on staying for dinner tonight. We can have another dinner when we get back. In fact, if you want, we can throw a big party. But tonight, I just want to celebrate with you."

I ran my fingers through his hair. "I've pinched myself multiple times today."

"It's real, Tessa. Some dreams come true." He pulled my

fingers to his lips. "What do you want our dream home to look like? I know it needs a gourmet kitchen and a hot tub."

"I'd love for it to have a rooftop patio." I brushed my lips on his scar. "And four or five bedrooms."

His fingers laced with mine.

"I've always thought I'd be a mom someday, but when I saw the way you were with Mason yesterday, I swooned a little. You'll be a great dad."

He sat up and held me to his chest. I knew what the compliment meant to him since he'd grown up away from his dad, but what I'd said was the absolute truth.

The sun sank toward the horizon as we cuddled and talked.

"If we're going to get married in an hour, I need to change clothes."

"You look beautiful just like you are."

"Thank you, but I want to wear a dress." I trailed a hand down the front of his shirt. "But I'll be really happy if you wear jeans."

Grinning, he nuzzled my neck. "Why is that?"

"Tonight, when I help you take them off, I won't have my eyes closed."

His laugh sounded almost like a growl. "On that note, I'm going to take you home and let you change."

While he packed up the blanket and cooler, I stared out at the view. Picking up a stranger had led to this. Not only had I found the man of my dreams, but this gorgeous place would be my home.

When we arrived at the cabins, he walked me to my door and snuck in one more peck before backing down the steps. "I'll be back here in thirty minutes."

"I'll be ready." I ran inside, and when I closed myself into the bedroom, I spotted a gift bag on the bed.

I opened the card, expecting that this was another

surprise from Garrett. But I was wrong. One of the risks of leaving my door unlocked was that I never knew when one of my friends would leave me a surprise.

Something for tonight. Enjoy! – Delaney

It wasn't hard to guess what was in the bag. I yanked out the tissue and smiled. Garrett had arranged for a lot of surprises, and thanks to Delaney, I'd have one of my own.

I hurriedly changed clothes, then stuffed what I needed for the next few days into a bag. Hopefully, I'd remembered everything important. I'd packed a toothbrush and my doughnut cutter. Other than that, what would I really need?

Standing in front of the mirror, I applied lipstick. The fear that had held me prisoner for so long was gone. In its place was anticipation and desire.

When I stepped outside, Garrett was already on the porch. "Let's go get married."

I handed him my bag, and he tossed it into the truck. Then he kissed me as I buckled my seat belt. Too much more of this, and we'd be late to our own wedding.

All the way to the main house, he held my hand, and that thumb brushed back and forth.

As he parked, I pulled his fingers to my lips. "I'm so excited."

"Me too." He ran around and helped me out of the truck, then stopped before opening the front door. "Last chance to change your mind."

"Okay. Well, I guess…" I crinkled my nose, pausing to build tension. "A party might be fun."

"I'll make sure to invite Nico." Garrett knew there was no reason to be jealous, but now it was a running joke.

"He was there when you proposed. And I'm pretty sure he has his sights on someone else."

"He does, and I'll tell you that story later. But I couldn't have told you who was in the shop." Garrett kissed me as he opened the door. "You were my focus. Then. Now. Always."

Our family and closest friends cheered as we walked into the house. There was standing room only in Beau and Lilith's great room.

Mad Dog stood by the back door, grinning from ear to ear. "I'm ready whenever y'all are."

I wasn't one of the girls who'd dreamed about the ideal wedding and planned most of it before meeting the groom, but the way this day had worked out, the small ceremony with only our family and closest friends around us, was perfect. Absolutely perfect.

My dad stepped next to me. "Tessa honey, you look just beautiful." He held out his arm. "I've been waiting for this."

"You knew he was going to propose today, didn't you?"

Dad shot a glance at Garrett. "We got the call yesterday, but we've been expecting it for about a month."

I grabbed Garrett's hand. "What am I missing?"

Dad chuckled. "Well, during your visit when I asked him what his intentions were, he said he intended to propose soon after you changed your mind about never risking your heart in a relationship again."

Garrett flashed his best smile. "I wasn't going to lie to your dad."

"You are totally worth the risk." I hugged him. "I'll meet you at the front."

After another quick kiss, my handsome cowboy spy strode to the front, then turned and smiled, his gaze fixed on me.

As my dad escorted me across the room, I admired Garrett. He was my happy now and my happily ever after. Risking my heart had gained me the whole world.

* * *

I HELD tight to Garrett's neck as he carried me into the house. He bumped the door closed with his hip, then turned so that I could flip the bolt.

"Our bags are in the bedroom." He brushed his lips on mine.

"What did you wish for?"

Curiosity wrinkled his brow. "What?"

"In the hot tub the night before Delaney's wedding. We saw a shooting star, and you said that soon you'd tell me about it. But you haven't."

"And you pick now to ask?" He glanced toward the hall.

It dawned on me that I might be getting heavy. "You can put me down. I'm sorry about making you hold me so long. But I am curious. Please tell me."

He shifted his hold but didn't put me down. "I wished that I'd get to redeem that other raincheck." With his eyebrows lifted, he looked toward the bedroom again. He didn't have to say the words out loud for me to understand his question.

I fingered a button on his shirt, anticipating how amazing it would feel to have him on top of me. "Take me to bed, cowboy."

"Yes, ma'am."

EPILOGUE

GARRETT

*L*eaning against the barn, I watched as Tessa rode up the path. Her hair blew in the breeze, and a wide smile stretched across her face. We'd been married eight months, and seeing her still made my heart pound faster.

Parker slapped my shoulder. "I'll let you help her down. Then I'll take care of Sprinkles."

"Thanks." I met Tessa just outside the corral. "Hello, gorgeous."

Her cheeks, still flushed from riding, changed from pink to red. "Hiya, cowboy." She dismounted and wrapped her arms around me. "I thought you'd be busy until later."

"You know what today is?" I picked her up, cradling her in my arms.

"Hmm. Monday?" She chewed her bottom lip. "Did I forget something important?"

"One year ago today, I asked you out, and you turned me down." I'd marked the date in my calendar shortly after she'd decided to risk being more than friends.

Her eyes widened. "Garrett!"

Chuckling, I carried her to the truck. "If you have time, I was hoping you'd spend the rest of the day with me."

"Now that I know what day it is, I can't exactly say no. Not that I would anyway." She grinned. "What do you have planned?"

"You'll see." I set her in the passenger seat.

She grabbed my shirt. "Do I need to change clothes?"

"You'll see." I loved watching her anticipation mount.

As I pulled away from the barn, I clasped her hand. "I ran into town this morning and bumped into someone at the feed store."

"Okay?"

"I'd never met him before, but he sure was eager to meet me. Went on about how he'd been friends with you years ago." I glanced at her to catch her reaction.

"Skeeter?" Panic flashed in her eyes.

"I didn't hurt him." That man's stupidity was why I'd gotten my happily ever after. "I'm glad you didn't end up with that guy." I winked. "For lots of reasons."

Her brown eyes twinkled. "Me too."

With her, the promises I'd made at the wedding—for better or for worse, for richer or poorer, in sickness and in health—were easy to say. I'd seen her character, and there wasn't anything I wouldn't do for her. She made me a better man. And she made me very, very happy.

I squeezed her hand as I turned out of the ranch. "They broke ground on the new cabins today. I hope this helps us hang on to some of these ranch hands."

"You can't blame them for falling in love." She danced her eyebrows. "It happens to the *best* of us."

"Right when we least expect it." Chuckling, I drove up to our hilltop. "The crew isn't working today, but I've been assured the house will be ready by Thanksgiving."

The crew wasn't working today because I'd requested the house be empty for my little surprise.

She pressed a hand to her chest. "I'm so excited."

"And while the house isn't quite finished, it's close enough for us to celebrate you turning me down with a soak in the hot tub."

"You make it sound horrible."

"I thought you liked the hot tub." I opened her door.

"Not as much as I like you." She fluttered her eyelashes.

"Well played." I lifted a small overnight bag out of the back seat. "You will need to change clothes... to what's in here."

She started to open the bag.

"No peeking. Just go change." I pushed open the front door. "But if you want to walk around and see the progress first, I'm fine with that."

Hand in hand, we wandered through the house, like we'd done at least once a week for the last several months. Tessa talked about where she wanted to put furniture, and I drank in her smile. My opinions on furniture placement wouldn't fill one page. Whatever she wanted was fine with me.

She tugged me to the patio door in the master bedroom. "Having a private patio out here is going to be awesome. I love that we decided to have the hot tub right outside our bedroom."

"Just like at the getaway house. Except this patio is only accessible from this room."

"Perfect. I love how the house is coming along. We should go pick out a table for the kitchen soon."

"We should." I pulled her close. "Why don't you change in here? Then I'll unveil the next part of my plan." I let my hands wander on her back and down over her jeans. "I'm thankful that our story didn't end in the doughnut shop that day."

Her eyes misted as she nodded.

"I'll be back in a few minutes." I pressed a kiss to her forehead before walking toward the door. "I hope you like what I bought."

The zipper slid open, and she gasped. "It's so tiny!"

Anticipating how she'd look in that new bikini, I ran up to the rooftop patio. On the last few tours of the house, I'd distracted her from coming up here.

Everything was ready. The wine was chilled and waiting within reach. The hot tub was bubbling. And the weather was perfect.

It wasn't as cold as last year, and I had no complaints about that.

After swapping my jeans and shirt for a swimsuit, I ran back downstairs and knocked on the bedroom door. "Did it fit?"

Laughter rang out. "See for yourself."

Grinning, I strolled into the room and was surprised to find her wearing the fuzzy robe. And it was tied closed. "Tease."

With the robe still closed, she grinned as she spun in a circle with her arms spread out. "It fits. Are you going to turn on the hot tub?"

"Nope. Come with me." I looped my pinkie around hers and led her through the house and up to the door that led out to the rooftop patio. "Close your eyes."

She squeezed them closed, then slapped a hand over her eyes for good measure. "They're closed."

I pushed open the door and guided her outside. "Have a look."

"Oh, wow!" Her smile widened as she scanned the patio. "I absolutely love the idea of having a hot tub on the rooftop patio. And you bought furniture." She stepped up to the porch rail. "The view is incredible, and it's so private." She slipped the robe off her shoulders and let it fall. "This was a fabulous idea."

"It was your idea. You mentioned it the first time I brought you up here." I traced her curves with my fingertips. "This string bikini was also a fabulous idea."

She turned around, her dark hair brushing her shoulders. "Let's not stay in the hot tub long."

"Fine with me." I stepped into the bubbling water, then held her hand as she joined me. "This is where I make a joke about pulling a few strings."

Laughing, she nestled into my lap. "I have no objections." She pressed a hand to my chest, then trailed her fingers across my skin. "And so far, I like your plan for the day."

"This is only just the beginning. Wine?"

Chewing her lip, she shook her head. "No thanks."

"Are you sure? Normally you..." A lightbulb exploded inside my head. "Are you..."

Tessa smiled. "Surprise."

BONUS EPILOGUE

ALMOST TWO YEARS LATER

ADAM

Butch bumped my leg, then barked before walking toward the guest room. I knew what that meant. Having well-trained dogs was almost like having a babysitter.

"He's in there again, isn't he?" I patted Butch's head, and he another bark.

The door was cracked, and I pushed it open the rest of the way. Sundance stood guard beside the boxes, watching as my three-year-old made his way up the cardboard mountain.

Sundance gave me an exhausted look.

I pulled Aiden off the stack of boxes and tickled him as I walked out of the room with the dogs on my heels. I closed the door to the guest room, thinking a doorknob with a lock would be a good investment. "Buddy, please stay off the boxes."

"I was climbing to the top of the building to save the people." Aiden wiggled, trying to get down. "Like you save people."

"Later, we can save the people together, but right now, we need to get ready for the party." I set him down. "Where are your shoes?"

"In the kitchen." He darted away before I could ask why his shoes were in the kitchen.

After moving into this house last week, it was a wonder he could find his shoes at all.

I leaned around the corner and called after him, "When you find them, let me help you put them on." I snapped and pointed down the hall. Butch and Sundance trotted toward the kitchen, earning their keep.

"I can do it." Aiden uttered those words about a hundred times a day.

Eve smiled when I stepped into our bedroom. "He was in the guest room again?"

"Saving people from the top of the building. I won't be surprised if one day, he has a fireman's hat and coat on Sundance. But as long as Aiden isn't trying to get on the roof, I can deal." I rubbed her tummy. "How are you feeling?"

"Huge. Remind me to plan better if we do this again. Being pregnant in August isn't fun." She fanned herself and glanced down at her shoes. "Would you mind—"

"Daddy, I need help. My shoes don't fit." Aiden crawled up on our bed and sat beside Eve. "Hi, Mommy."

"Hey, sweetheart. Are you ready to eat brisket?"

I knelt next to the bed and switched Aiden's shoes so that they were on the correct feet. "I'm ready for brisket."

"Aunt Haley said if I eat the meat, then I can have a roasted marshmallow." He grinned. "And she said Uncle Zach makes good meat."

"She's right." I massaged Eve's feet one at a time, only for a minute or so.

She sighed. "That feels amazing."

"I'll give you a better foot rub later tonight." I slipped on her shoes. "Are we ready to go?"

She nodded as she pushed off the bed. "I'm so glad for the timing of this move." Tears welled up in her eyes. "Having everyone close feels so good."

I hugged her, not as bothered by her misty eyes. Tears were much more common when she was pregnant.

"Me too." I picked up Aiden. "Let's load up."

When we stepped outside, Eve looked down the street. "Driving seems silly, but I doubt I can walk two blocks in this heat."

I buckled Aiden into his seat. "Driving is better because when we leave, someone might be T I R E D."

Aiden cocked his head. "Daddy, why did you say letters?"

"You'll get to see Hannah Jo today. Won't that be fun?" Eve knew when to change the subject.

My kid scrunched up his nose. "She's kinda little. But Uncle Hank will play with me."

"Kinda little, huh? She's only a few months younger than you are, bud. But I'm sure Uncle Hank will play with you." I ran back to the front door. "You boys, be good. Maybe you can talk Pookie into coming out from under our bed. I bet you can sweet-talk her, Sundance."

He gave a short bark.

"Great. See y'all later." I locked the door, then climbed into the driver's seat.

After driving one block, I turned and passed five houses before stopping in front of Zach and Haley's place.

Buying a house so close to Eve's best friend was one of the best decisions Eve and I had ever made. I'd feel better when I worked nights, knowing that she had friends close.

Zach stepped out and waved. On each hip was a grinning toddler. "Come on in. Haley's in the kitchen."

CJ sat on the front step, his tail swinging back and forth.

Aiden ran up and stopped, his brow furrowed. "When are your boys going to be big so they can play?"

Zach laughed. "It's hard being the oldest, isn't it? CJ will play with you."

Aiden took off into the house with the dog right behind. It was nice having other adults around.

"Take your time. I'll watch him." Zach sauntered inside.

Holding Eve's hand, I kept my pace slow. "Once we're inside, find a seat, and then I'll grab you something to drink." I kissed her hand. "And when we get home, you can relax in a bubble bath."

She rolled her eyes. "If I climbed into the tub now, I'd need a rescue just to get out."

I slipped my arms around her. "I know just the man for the job."

ZACH

The boys giggled as they watched Aiden run around with CJ. I'd gotten the dog because of his name, and he'd turned out to be amazing, one of the best dogs I'd ever met.

"Let's go on outside." I barely had the back door open before Aiden was barreling through.

There wasn't a fire in the pit. That would have to wait until there were more dads around to stand guard and until I had a free hand. With the twins, getting things done required ingenuity.

I set them in their playpen and scooted it so that they were out of the sun but could be entertained by CJ and Aiden playing. Then I checked the brisket.

"Is it ready?" Haley brushed curls out of her face. "I have the fries in the oven and the veggie tray prepped."

"It's ready to come off. Mind watching the fellas? We've

added one." I pointed at the playpen. "Happiness in confinement will be short lived."

She rubbed my back, pretending like she wasn't sniffing my shirt. "I can't believe they're almost two. And watching Aiden, I know we'll blink, and the boys will be starting kindergarten."

I tugged at one of the curls that had fallen out of her messy bun. "Yep. Hopefully, Clint and Joji will still babysit for us then."

She inched up and kissed me. "I hope so too. They are watching them tomorrow night. All night."

The lid to the barbecue pit slammed down when I spun around to look at her. "I didn't know. I haven't made any reservations or booked us a place."

"Careful with that lid." She made a show of sniffing my shirt. "I made all the arrangements. We're going camping." Her eyebrows danced as she blew me a kiss.

"We'll pack itch cream and tweezers just in case." I received the expected eye roll as a reply. "Love you."

"I know you do." She leaned over the playpen. "How are my boys? Are you having fun watching Aiden?"

Josh held onto the side and did his impression of a kangaroo. Jeremy held up his arms, wanting freedom.

She laughed. "I'll get you out, but stay by Mommy."

I carried the brisket inside and wrapped it in foil. Once the timer was set, I made sure the coolers had ice and that everything in the kitchen was ready and childproof.

Life had changed from when we had a bunch of singles hanging out on the patio.

When a knock sounded, I skirted around the living room, letting Adam and Eve have a few more uninterrupted seconds.

I pulled open the door, and Hannah Jo ran right past me.

Nacha shook her head. "I'm sorry. She's been talking

about Aiden and the twins all day." She darted off after her daughter.

Hank swung the door closed after stepping inside. "I may need to have a talk with Adam. Hannah Jo is talking about Aiden a lot."

"Easy there, Hank. She's three." I enjoyed poking fun at my friend.

"Guys are never too young to treat a girl nicely." He waved at Adam and Eve. "I was kidding about Aiden and Hannah Jo."

Adam laughed. "I gathered that. I should probably go check on him. He's on a rescuing kick. We might find him on the roof or find your cat bandaged."

"And that could be dangerous." I peeked outside. "The roof would be bad too."

Hank laughed. "Y'all sit. Nacha and I will wrangle kids for a bit."

"And Haley is out there." I opened the cooler. "Something to drink?"

"Anything with caffeine." Hank accepted a Pepsi before walking out the door.

Even as different as things were, I loved entertaining, and Haley seemed to enjoy it as much as I did.

She hadn't given me much notice on the camping trip, but I'd figure out some way to surprise her. Standing by the window, I watched as she chased Aiden and Hannah Jo around the yard while the boys rolled in the grass, playing with CJ. That dog earned his keep a hundred times over.

I looked down when something bumped my leg. "Waldo, you stupid cat. Drop that bra right now."

Waldo raced into the living room with the bra strap between his teeth, the rest of the bra flapping behind him.

The worst part, that cat always ruined my favorites.

The back door opened, and Waldo slipped outside. Being

out there with all the kids served him right. I hoped Aiden would catch the cat and wrap him in gauze. We probably had a few rolls around here somewhere.

HANK

Thanks to that stupid cat, I'd seen more of my sister's underwear than I'd ever wanted to see. I stomped on the end of the lacy thing, and the cat jerked backward before darting toward the fence. "Zach, if you want it, grab it. I'm not touching it."

"Why am I not surprised?" Laughing, Zach shoved the bra partially into his pocket. "I'm going to make this disappear."

"You do that." I smiled when I felt a small tug on my pant leg. "Hello, princess."

Hannah Jo held up a bean bag and pointed at the Corn Hole game. "Play with me."

I picked her up as she brushed dark strands out of her face. She was a miniature of her mother. Beautiful.

"Sure thing. Should we ask Aiden to play too?"

She bobbed her head. "He'll play with you. You're big."

"I bet he'll play with you too."

Looking across the yard, she shrugged.

"Hannah Jo, come over here. Aiden wants to play Corn Hole with you." Haley waved from the yard.

Hannah Jo wiggled, trying to get down. "Put me down, Daddy."

"Do you want me to play with you?"

Her pigtails swung side to side as she shook her head. Her feet barely touched the ground, and she was off like a shot.

"She only wanted me to play when she thought Aiden didn't want to play." I didn't expect anyone to respond to my complaint, but I said it just the same.

Nacha rubbed my back. "I still love you." She slipped her arms around my waist. "And good catch back there."

I nuzzled her neck. "I'd prefer to see someone else's bra."

She propped her fists on her hips, leaving a cold spot where she'd been hugging me. "Whose bra?" Her voice was firm, but her dark eyes sparkled.

"Or maybe that little bikini you wore the night you saved me in the pool." I dropped kisses on her neck.

"Y'all need us to watch Hannah Jo tonight?" Clint laughed as he wandered toward the Corn Hole game.

"Papa Clint!" Hannah Jo dropped her bean bag and darted toward him.

I pulled Nacha's arms around me. "I love that she has your mom, Mateo, and Clint and Joji."

"Me too. And I'll check with Joji, but if they don't mind, Hannah Jo can sleep over there. And then my bikini might make an appearance."

I pressed my hands together. "Please. Oh please."

"I'm going to take some pictures."

"These are definitely times we'll want to remember, and because of our complete exhaustion, pictures are our only hope of remembering." I kissed her.

"I'll remember. There are details I'll forget, but I'll remember being happy." She cupped my cheek. "Very, very happy."

The back door opened, and I glanced over. "Aunt Joji!"

Nacha squatted, smiling. "Alyssa, look at how big you are!"

Cami's daughter toddled beside Joji, holding her hand.

"She's almost as tall as you are, Aunt Joji." I stepped behind Nacha just in case Aunt Joji didn't find my comment humorous.

She stuck her tongue out at me.

"Hey, we don't want the kids learning that behavior." I feigned disappointment.

She shook her head. "Go make yourself useful. Cami wanted ice cream."

"How much did Harper buy?" I ran through the house and met him at the front door. "Is this all for Cami?"

He handed me several bags. "She'll probably share. Take these. I'll get the toppings."

HARPER

As I reached into the trunk, Adam walked up beside me. "How often do y'all have these big get-togethers?" He loaded his arms with bags.

"Sometimes we skip a few months. Other times, we meet up every few weeks. It just depends on who has sick kids and what the weather's like." I closed the trunk. "Y'all will love it here."

"I think we will. Eve is already happier, and we've only been here a week. I think this still feels like her hometown." He shoved the front door open. "How are y'all?"

I hadn't had an extended conversation with my best friend in weeks. We'd helped them the weekend they'd moved in, but he and I hadn't gotten more than a few minutes to talk. Even then, we were chasing kids.

Grinning, I kept my voice low. "Really good. It's not public yet, but we have another one on the way."

Adam shook his head. "In a few years, we can start our own baseball team."

"Or tee ball. Then we wouldn't have to wait so long." I dumped the bags on the empty counter. "I hope Hank put the ice cream where it won't melt. Keep the sweets away from the edge. Alyssa has taken to walking through the kitchen attempting to snag stuff off the counters. It's great fun."

Cami's laugh echoed from the living room. The sheer joy of the sound always made me smile.

"When is your first day?" I pushed all the jars toward the back of the counter, then set the whipped cream in the fridge.

Adam crossed his arms and leaned back against the counter. "Monday. I'm glad it worked out to change departments."

I patted his arm. "Yeah. Maybe working together, we'll get to talk once in a while." I fished a bottle of water out of the cooler, then nodded toward the living room.

Adam followed as I walked toward our wives.

"Where's Alyssa?" I scanned the room, ready to launch into a search.

Cami slipped an arm around me. "With Joji. You can relax."

I dropped into the overstuffed chair and tugged her into my lap. "I'm trusting there are enough adults out there to keep kids alive."

"Hope so!" She pulled my arms around her. "Eve, do you remember Tessa? I know you went to school here. I think she's a bit younger than you and Haley."

Eve nodded. "I think so. Dark hair? Wasn't her last name something like…"

"Best." Cami nodded. "I'm sure she was never teased about that. Anyway, she'll be here. She runs the doughnut shop. They have a little guy who is maybe six months younger than Alyssa. Jack is a doll."

Eve smiled at Adam. "I don't know why we waited so long to move."

Cami grinned. "We're glad you finally did."

Sipping water, I enjoyed the quiet moment before I had to take a shift corralling kids.

The door opened, and we all looked that direction.

ELI

As I stepped into Zach and Haley's, Trixie leaned her head on my shoulder.

Delaney rubbed our daughter's back. "Daddy's got you, baby."

"She'll warm up." I kissed Delaney on the forehead. "You visit. I'll take her outside with the other kids."

She inhaled but nodded. "I have her bag if she needs anything."

Leaning close, I let my stubble brush Delaney's cheek. "I promise not to lose her."

"I didn't think that." She kissed me. "Just holler if you need anything."

Waving, I scanned the room. "Howdy!"

Cami pointed at the couple on the sofa. "Eli, Delaney, this is Adam and his wife Eve. They just moved in down the street."

Delaney extended her hand. "Haley's friend, right?"

Eve smiled as she rubbed her stomach. "Yes, and Adam and Harper have been friends for years."

"You look familiar. Are you from here?" I adjusted Trixie, making sure her little dress wasn't riding up.

"I am. Graduated the same year as Haley."

"Nice to have you back in town. I'm going to head outside and say hi to Zach and Haley." I walked out the back door, and Trixie clung to me tighter. "Sweetheart, you're fine. Look, there's Josh and Jeremy. And Alyssa and Hannah Jo."

Joji rubbed her hands together as she walked over. "How's my little Trixie?"

"Not sure she's in the mood to be passed around. She's been a bit clingy the last few days."

Joji lifted her eyebrows. "Really? There is an old wives' tale about that."

"Shh. We aren't making it public until Delaney's farther along." I hadn't planned to tell a soul, but Joji could keep a secret better if she knew it was a secret.

Trixie's weight shifted, and I adjusted my hold so she wouldn't fall out of my arms. Then I realized the reason for her wiggles. She leaned toward Clint, her arms out.

He smiled. "Mind if I hold her?"

"Not at all." I handed Trixie over.

Joji pointed toward the door. "Can I grab you a drink? Where's Sherlock?"

"Keeping up with one is hard enough right now. Sherlock and CJ can play later. And yes, anything cold is great." I walked out to the Corn Hole game where a rather chaotic version was being played. The kids pelted bean bags at the holes and sometimes at Zach. He shielded himself and ran in circles, which drew giggles.

Haley hugged me. "We haven't seen y'all in over a week. How's life?"

"Tiring. But good." I watched as her two guys chased their dad. "But not as tiring as yours, I'm guessing."

She nodded. "I love it though."

That was obvious.

Joji handed me a water, then joined Clint and Trixie. A couple with no kids, they were grandparents to an entire brood. And the kids loved them.

When I heard a door slam, I peeked around the side of the house. Garrett helped Tessa out of the truck, then pulled open the back door.

Since marrying my cousin, he'd become one of my closest friends.

I motioned to Clint and Joji that I was headed inside, then I walked through the house to greet Garrett and Tessa.

As I walked up, Jack stretched out, wanting me to hold him.

246

"Hey there, big guy." I pulled him into my arms. "I hear you're walking."

"Barely." Tessa sighed. "We've had a lot of topples this week."

Garrett grinned. "I wasn't prepared for how things would change once he became mobile."

"Don't tell me. I'd rather live in my bubble a little longer and just be surprised." I carried Jack toward the house. "Maybe if we're lucky, Trixie won't walk until she's sixteen."

"Right before she learns to drive." Garrett slapped me on the back. "Great plan."

GARRETT

I caught Tessa's hand as Eli carried Jack inside. "Quick, let's get in the truck. They'll take care of him."

She slipped her arms around my waist. "Funny. Maybe we'll have to see if Lilith and your dad want to keep Jack one night soon. They've offered more than once, and I think our hot tub feels neglected."

"Not just the hot tub." I winked, knowing she would understand my humor. "Do you know who all is supposed to be here today?"

"Haley's friend Eve and her husband just moved to town. The rest of the group is here. Joji and Clint. And I think Cami invited Tandy, then talked Zach into inviting his granddad. I'm not sure how that will play out." She crinkled her nose. "They hate each other, but Cami seems determined. Or maybe she doesn't know that."

I blinked. "Tandy? Is she that author woman?"

"You know her?"

"Oh, I've met her. She asked me to remove my clothing, then acted like she was going to remove hers. She may have been pulling my leg, but keep her far away from me."

Tessa laughed. "I'll keep her away. I'm the only one who gets to make that request." She squeezed my hand. "Oh! The doughnuts. I created a new flavor. S'mores."

"Yum. That sounds good." I grabbed them out of the back seat.

She caught my free hand. "I wasn't sure if Zach was going to risk starting a fire, so just in case, I made those. They have marshmallow cream and graham cracker bits on top of the chocolate doughnuts."

"Maybe I'll just roast a doughnut over the fire." I kissed her hand before shoving open the door. "I'll find Jack and make sure he's good."

"Thanks, love."

"Hello, all!" I waved, then dropped the doughnuts onto the counter before wandering out to the backyard.

Jack toddled near the Corn Hole game, and Eli tossed the bean bag before handing one to Jack, but he wasn't interested in the game. Jack wanted to play with the dog.

CJ lay down, and Jack buried his face in the dog's fur, giggling.

Eli glanced back. "Maybe y'all need one of these."

"Why? They have one. You have one. And I don't have to clean up poo. Dog poo, at least."

He laughed.

"Although, the other day, I came home to find Blue sleeping on our couch. For someone who was determined not to get a dog, Tessa has bonded with that one." I didn't want to think about how old Blue was. Maybe he'd just live forever. "I heard Tandy and your granddad were coming today."

Eli blinked. "For real? Not together."

"Cami seems to think they are meant for each other."

"I think they're like fire and gasoline." He rubbed the back of his neck. "We'll see how it goes, I guess."

"Tessa mentioned y'all had a secret."

Eli's head bobbed. "Just when we were getting the hang of things, we're going to get double teamed."

"Y'all will be great. And you know we're happy to babysit whenever. Seriously. You know that, right?" I picked up Jack as he toddled toward me.

"I do." Eli glanced back at the door. "Uh-oh. She's here. Want to wager on how long it takes her to ask one of us to take off our shirt?"

"Tessa promised to keep her away from me. And that's only one of the reasons I love my wife."

TANDY

I wasn't sure how I'd managed an invitation to the barbecue, but it was a welcome change from sitting alone in front of my computer. At home, I didn't have anyone to talk to except my characters.

My choices had led to these quiet years, but the past couldn't be changed. I'd learned to live with that.

The energy with all the young couples and their kiddos was electric. Watching them fed my soul. Later at home, I'd write for hours, inspired by this energy. I sipped my wine cooler, studying the guys and working through descriptions in my head.

These men had grown into wonderful fathers, and it was fun watching them playing with their kids and doting on their wives.

But with so many of them happily married, I was running out of people to tease about posing.

I sensed Matthew Gallagher before I noticed him.

"They're all happily married. You'll have to find someone else to play cougar with." He leaned against the wall next to me and tipped his beer bottle as a sort of greeting.

Matthew Gallagher was as maddening as ever.

Under my breath, I called him a bad word.

He touched a finger to his lips. "You don't want the little ones hearing that kind of talk."

"Shut up." I hated that after more than forty years, I still felt the pull of attraction to the man.

"Since we haven't spoken in a while, I thought I'd say hello and make conversation."

"A while? It's been decades." I folded my arms and blew out a frustrated breath.

He leaned down, those green eyes that God had blessed all those Gallagher men with boring right through me. "I know how long it's been, Tandy."

"We talked. Do you feel better now?"

"Not yet." He tipped his cowboy hat. "Nice to see you."

It was the first time we'd talked in decades, and he'd called me a cougar. That snark was why I hadn't spoken to him in so long. One of the reasons. The other reason was more uncomfortable. Regret.

But one thing was for sure. I'd never give Matthew Gallagher the chance to break my heart again.

A NOTE TO READERS

Thank you for reading! When Wrangled by Lilith released, I had readers ask if Garrett would get a story. I knew his story would be part of this series, but until Cami's book, I wasn't sure who his perfect person would be.

Be sure to check out my website at www.PhreyPress.com for information about upcoming releases and to find other sweet romances and romcoms. To get updates in your inbox, subscribe to Remi's News. I also like to send my subscribers bonus and exclusive content.

ALSO BY REMI CARRINGTON

Never Say Never

Three Things I'd Never Do
One Guy I'd Never Date
Two Words I'd Never Say Again
One Choice I'd Never Make
Three Rules I'd Never Break
Two Risks I'd Never Take Again
One Whopper of a Love Story
Christmas Love
Christmas Sparkle
Christmas Surprise

Stargazer Springs Ranch
Fall in love with cowboys and spunky women.

Cowboys of Stargazer Springs
The ranch hands are falling in love.

Bluebonnets & Billionaires series
Lots of money & even more swoon.

Pamela Humphrey, who writes as Remi Carrington, also releases books under her own name. Visit PhreyPress.com for more information about her books.

ABOUT THE AUTHOR

Remi Carrington is a figment of Pamela Humphrey's imagination. She loves romance & chocolate, enjoys disappearing into a delicious book, and considers people-watching a sport. She was born in the pages of the novel *Just You* and then grew into an alter ego.

She writes sweet romance set in Texas. Her books are part of the Phrey Press imprint.

facebook.com/remiromance
instagram.com/phreypress

Printed in Great Britain
by Amazon